You Met Me
for a Reason

You Met Me
for a Reason

BHARGAV JARIWALA

White Falcon
Publishing

www.whitefalconpublishing.com

You Met Me for a Reason
Bhargav Jariwala

www.whitefalconpublishing.com

The contents of this book have been certified and timestamped on
the POA Network blockchain as a permanent proof of existence.
Scan the QR code or visit the URL given on the back cover to
verify the blockchain certification for this book.

Requests for permission should be addressed to
bhargavjariwala@yahoo.com

ISBN - 978-1-63640-488-2

Disclaimer

This novel is based on true events but all characters in the story are fictitious. Certain long-standing institutions, incidents and public places are mentioned, but they are totally imaginary. Any resemblance to anyone or anything is purely coincidental.

Inspired by people I once trusted blindly

There is always a reason we meet someone

Contents

1 Lost in Thoughts 1

2 The Second Met 9

3 The Journey Has Just Begun 18

4 'Trekking' – Experience of a Lifetime 28

5 Change in Behaviour 39

6 The Cozy Night 52

7 Past 66

8 Jealousness 81

9 First Date 95

10 Somewhere everyone is broken 104

11 Our First Kiss 113

12 Until Tomorrow 126

13   A Mysterious Truth.....................................138

14   Sour Tal Lake..147

15   The Proposal..154

16   Daily Casual Meets.....................................166

17   The Last Confession....................................173

18   The Wedding..185

You Met Me for a Reason.................................195

Acknowledgement...201

1

Lost in Thoughts

It was a hot sweaty night in the month of May. I sat on the bench staring at the huge round clock on Platform No. 2. A loud sound reverberated throughout the railway station when the clock struck 8 pm. I looked away from the clock to stare fixedly at the empty railway tracks in front of me, my forlorn eyes showing signs of emptiness. My heart was brimming with excitement, but my face looked tired and weary. I was feeling happy and dejected, both at the same time. Though eager for the upcoming adventure, I was depressed about the happenings in my personal life over the last few days. After staring at the tracks incessantly and swinging my legs back and forth in the air, I glanced around to see all that was taking place.

There was a mad rush on the platform with people hustling and bustling. Overcrowded and crammed with too many hawkers, coolies and families, it was far from the serenity I wished for at this point. Hawkers were shouting at the top of their voices, marketing their products. Porters were jostling and pushing, bargaining in loud voices with their customers. People were hurrying with their double baggage - their kids and the luggage. Due to the vacation time, it looked as if every family in the city was going on a holiday. There were people and bags and more people and more bags everywhere. It looked like a mini fun-fair, just minus the rides.

I was waiting, Lost in my own thoughts.

I noticed passer-by gawking at me as if I was an alien on the platform. Wearing loose baggy grey track pants and a neon-coloured graphic printed T-shirt, with a large backpack, and long hair for a boy, I looked somewhat like a hippie.

Normally, I considered myself a regular boy next door. But my family members thought otherwise. They always insisted that there was something about me that drew people towards me. With toffee-coloured brown eyes, a contagious smile, a sharp nose, square jaws and floppy hair which fell just past my chin, they considered me good-looking. I was always lively, full of zest and made friends easily. I was always the go-to person for any problems my friends and family encountered. Friends envied my face, they said I had a spark of mischief in my eyes and a heart of gold. But lately, they were all complaining about how my eyes spoke differently now. The spark was missing. The friendly smile had disappeared. No one knew that my heart held a story of deep pain. Yes, lately my behaviour had changed. I had become quiet. It was more like a conscious choice to be reserved, to stay away from people and their conversations. I did not feel like talking to anyone.

My thoughts were interrupted by a commotion from a small group of boys standing a few metres from me. Like me, they were dressed in tracks and tees with heavy backpacks. So here they are, I thought to myself. One of the boys from the group came up to me. He was carrying a big, bright orange rucksack on his shoulders and a large shopping bag in his left hand. He looked bewildered and curious. Anxiously, he asked me, "Trekking?" Before I could reply, he blurted out a storm of sentences. "Actually, this is my first trip though we are all travelling in a group. We were informed to come to platform 2. But we can't find our trekking sir. Would you mind telling us where the coach number of the train is displayed?" he said while showing me his ticket.

I remained silent, as this over-anxious person had disturbed my solitude. Instead of answering his questions, I just pointed to the blinking LED board on top which showed the coach numbers. This guy was visibly astonished by my behaviour and replied, "Ok, I knew that but was just confirming. Anyways, thanks buddy." He turned around to the two guys standing away and signalled them to come and join us. They all seemed clueless. Meanwhile this guy extended his right hand and said cheerfully, "Hi! I am Lakshya".

I shook his hand and replied, "Hello, I am Rihen".

He again started chattering. "I am so excited about the journey ahead. By the way, this is my first time on a trekking trip. And my mother has packed so much food," he said, pointing to the big carry bag in his left hand. "Rihen, is this your first trip too?" I could see excitement and confusion in his black hooded eyes.

"This is my second trip," I replied, to the point. I was not in the mood for a chit-chat right then. Thankfully, before he could continue with his volley of questions, the other boys arrived. We exchanged quick Hi's and Hello's and I shook hands with each of them. I noticed that everybody was in high spirits. Maybe, I too, needed to perk up my dull and serious face. Soon we heard a clear loud voice call out, "Sour Tal Lake Group, come over here please".

We all headed in the direction of the loud coarse voice. A tall, sturdy man with an exceptionally commanding presence was waving to us. Wearing a body-hugging T-shirt, blue shorts, a fit-bit watch, and sports shoes too big for his size, he looked almost ready to start an expedition. Our in-charge for the trekking trip, Raju Sir standing 6-ft tall had a towering personality in many ways. He had led many teams on trekking trips and had a great command over the groups. His stern face seemed intimidating, yet there was an aura of pleasantness which charmed many. Actually, he was the one who had motivated me to go on my first trekking trip. All four of us went to where he was standing. I went ahead of them to greet Sir personally, as I had known him since my previous trekking trip. Then, too, he was our coach and we had got quite close during that time. Raju Sir was standing with a pen and a sheaf of papers in his hand. He smiled upon seeing me. After a brief exchange of warm greetings, he asked me to stand with the group. I followed his instructions. From now on we all had to follow whatever Raju Sir told us.

Our train was on time, unlike the usual delay of trains in India. As soon as it came to a halt on the platform, our group started assembling their luggage. There was a lot of commotion on the platform. Some were shouting for their bags, others were waving to their families while Sir was trying to manage everyone. Getting on the train with so many members and luggage was a herculean task. But we finally managed to do so. Whoaaa... we all heaved a sigh of relief and settled down in our compartment. All the members smiled at each other, some giggled and some were counting & rechecking their luggage. Sir was still checking on everyone.

I found my seat by the window and quietly went there and settled down. I was trying to avoid all the hoo-ha in the train. I looked out of the window. The sky was pitch-black and not a star was visible. I was in a nonchalant mood, aloof to the enthusiasm of the other group members. Yes, I was happy to go on the trekking trip. I loved going to hill stations. Once a year, I made sure to travel to a place I hadn't visited before. So, it's always a new place, a new destination for me. Travelling thrills me.

So yes, here I was, on my way to a seven days trekking trip to Sour Tal (3,700-m) Lake (a group of frozen mountain tarns), in Manali district of Himachal Pradesh. This was my second trekking trip in one and a half years. We were travelling by train from Surat to Chandigarh and would later go by bus to Manali. This trek was graded easy-to-moderate and was exclusively for amateurs. This was one of the few unexplored, lesser known, spectacular and impressive treks of Kullu valley. Sir had told me that it was a very scenic, yet challenging summer high-altitude trek. I was excited about this daunting adventure and wanted to escape from the recent happenings in my life. My first trekking was a fun trip with my friends to Saputara, near Dang.

Normally, people liked to travel with friends and family, people they know and are familiar with. Earlier, even I did. But this time I decided to travel alone with complete strangers, who did not know me. I didn't wish for anyone's company. All I craved was for some ME time.I wanted to be by myself. To do whatever I liked. But amidst all this, something was bothering me. Something was hurting me from within. I tried to push away those thoughts.

"Dinner", one of the boys shouted, interrupting my thoughts.

I suddenly realized how hungry I was.

"Coming", I told him.

I took out my disposable food packet, lovingly packed by my mother, and went to the adjacent compartment. The aroma of home food filled my nostrils and added fuel to my hunger pangs. All the group members were seated haphazardly in an uneven circle. They had kept all the food in the middle of the lower berth on some newspapers. I somehow pushed myself into a corner of the lower seat and almost gobbled down my food. Damn, I didn't realize how hungry I was.

After dinner, Raju Sir went back to his seat, but everyone else stayed there and warmed up to each other. There was an exchange of introductions and friendly banter. Slowly the discussion moved from family details to love for travelling to entertainment and ended up with everyone singing songs at a high pitch.

I was oblivious to all this, lost in my own world. At around 10.30 pm I said bye to everyone and went off to sleep.

'Chai garam chai'...

The loud hoarse voice of the *chaiwalas* woke me up the next morning.

It was 7.00 am.

Being summer time, the sun was already up in the sky casting its golden rays through the window on my face. I opened my eyes partly to look outside the window. We were passing through a small village it seemed. Others were still sleeping. After a while I went back to sleep again.

It was almost 10.00 am by the time I got up next. I glanced around. Most of the members were now awake. There was a rush for the washroom. I quickly got up to brush and freshen up. I heard someone saying that late in the night, few more members from Vadodara and Ahmedabad had boarded the train and joined our group.

"Hey, are you Rihen?", one of the boys shouted at me.

"Yes, I am Rihen," I answered while still brushing my teeth. "Why?" I asked, the foam of the toothpaste almost coming out of my mouth.

"Raju Sir is looking for you", he shouted back.

"Ok, I will go and meet him after I'm done here," I replied back.

After I finished brushing and my daily morning routine, I went towards Raju Sir's compartment.

"Good morning, Sir," I greeted him as soon as I saw him.

"Morning, Rihen. I need your help to prepare and distribute the food packages to our team in an hour.

"Sure Sir, I would be more than happy to help," I said with a slight smile.

Till then he wanted to discuss a few things about our trip. Since he knew me well, he thought I would be able to help him. I readily agreed to assist him during the course. First, we made a list of the participants. Then we checked the first-aid kits and other equipment.

Once this was done, I helped Sir to pack the food packages for all our group members. In turn, he gave me a list of the seat numbers and member names, giving clear instructions to personally hand over the food packets and tick the members on the list.

I looked down at the list, there were 21 names on it. Of these, 11 were from Vadodara, 6 from Ahmedabad and 4 from Surat. I started as per the given list. First, I distributed the packages amongst the Surat and Vadodara members. Most of them were awake by now and thanked me for the food packets, some even smiled at me. After having distributed the packets to them, I ticked their names on the list.

Now it was the turn of the Ahmedabad members.

When I went to their compartment, I found that all except one girl were up. I distributed the packets as per the list. Now only one girl remained. The name on the list read Naira.

2

The Second Met

Naira. The name struck a chord with me. It seemed quite familiar, but I just couldn't recall where I had heard it.

Perplexed I asked, "Where is Naira?" The others pointed towards the upper berth where a girl was still sleeping peacefully. Since the AC was on, she was wrapped under the bulky warm blanket except for her white slender legs which were slightly visible beneath the sheets. I tapped her legs gently "Hey Naira, I have got your food packet.", "Keep it on my bag," she said sleepily from beneath her blanket and pointed to a bag next to her legs. I did just that. I was still scratching my head, wondering where on earth I had heard this sweet voice. With one more glance at the sleeping figure, I went out of the compartment to hand over the list to Raju Sir.

It was almost late evening when we reached Chandigarh. When we assembled on the platform, Raju Sir shouted loud and clear, "Everyone here?"

"Yes," everyone said quietly.

"Are you all still sleeping? I can't hear you, Sir replied annoyingly. "All here?" he asked again loudly.

"Yes Sir, this time everyone answered vociferously.

Then Sir gave us a few instructions to follow throughout our journey from Chandigarh to Manali.

"There are three groups - from Ahmedabad, Vadodara and Surat. If someone is missing from your group, you have to immediately report to me.

"Everyone has to maintain discipline and always be on time.

"Now we will board a bus to Manali. Take your seats in that bus, and after an hour we will stop at a *dhaba* (a small roadside food outlet) for dinner. Then we will directly stop at Manali. Since you are going to spend the night in the bus, keep your handbags and woolen clothes with you and give your main bags to the bus conductor. After that, you will get your main bags only at Manali. So, take out whatever you might need right now. Later on, I don't want any excuses."

After he finished giving the instructions, he again shouted, "Group, is everything clear?"

"Yes Sir," everyone replied in unison.

We were all eagerly looking forward to our trekking trip.

"So get ready and let's go," Sir said.

We all started towards our bags to take out the things we thought we might need during our bus journey, and then sat in the bus. It was time for our adventure to begin...

So here we were...All set for an immensely unnerving and high-octane adventure. Everyone was flushed with excitement.

We all were very enthusiastic and looking forward to our seven days trek. As anyone who has been on a trekking expedition would agree, it was going to be an experience of a lifetime. A story, I'm sure, we wouldn't mind repeating again and again to others.

The bus started for Manali at 7 pm. I was sitting with Raju Sir on the opposite side of the driver's seat. After two hours, the bus stopped at a small *dhaba* for dinner. As soon as we got down from the bus, a smoky aroma filled our nostrils titillating our empty stomachs. We were all starved and the smell of the delicious food made us even more hungry.

While having dinner, I noticed a pretty girl continuously staring at me. When I looked towards her, she gave me a broad smile, her cute dimples adorning her pink cheeks. But I didn't smile back because even though she seemed familiar, I couldn't recall her. She was still gazing in my direction. I was a bit astonished by her behavior. I couldn't figure out why this unknown girl was constantly looking at me. Yes, the face somewhat did appear familiar to me. But I couldn't remember ever having seen her. I tried to ignore her by focusing on my dinner. But soon enough, I saw her coming towards me. I got nervous. Why was she staring at me like that? And why was she coming in my direction?

Before she could reach me, I quickly got up and went hastily towards the washroom. I thought this was a good escape plan and would drive her away from me.

But when I came back to my seat, she was already there talking with Raju Sir.

"Hey Rihen, I am Naira," She extended her hand towards me.

'Ohh, she's the same girl who was sleeping in the train's compartment when I went there to give breakfast. And she knows my name,' I muttered to myself.

"Hi," I said blankly and shook her hand for a fraction of a second. Without a blink, she said, "I forgot to take out my jacket from my bag which is on the roof of the bus. Can you please help me get it out? I am feeling cold."

'Why me?' Again, I wondered to myself.

My face was as cold as a stone. I stood there expressionless, not knowing what to say. I looked at her. She stood before me, looking innocently at me. On a dark night like this, the moon was shining brightly, illuminating her rosy face like a ball of light. Her pink, delicate lips just below her slight, buttoned nose displayed a dimpled smile. Her cute dimple cheeks enthralled me. Her wavy dark brown hair with soft curls cascaded down her beautiful face. Fair, pretty and dimple faced, she looked quite familiar. But at this point my mind was blank. I couldn't recall where I had seen this attractive face before. This lovely girl wanted me to help her take out her jacket.

When I didn't reply, she turned her face towards Raju Sir and requested him again. "Raju Sir, I am sorry I didn't follow your instructions. But I am feeling cold and as I told you I forgot my jacket in my main bag and now I want it," she said apologetically.

"I had informed everyone beforehand to take out all the necessary stuff from your main bags," Sir said annoyingly.

"I know Sir, and I am very sorry. But please help me as its very cold out here," she pleaded again.

"Okay, Rihen help her out, Sir told me. I was just about to refuse when Sir gave me a beseeching look.

"Come, let's go," I told her in an irritated tone. I was displeased with Sir's order to help this insane yet beautiful girl. But she ignored my resentment. Instead there was a deep grin on her face. It seemed she was smiling to herself, her adorable dimples clearly visible on her pink cheeks.

"You remember me, right?" Naira asked me as soon as the two of us were alone. There was a faraway look in her deep brown dusty eyes. They were piercing right through my mind.

"No, I don't remember," I said abruptly and started walking faster towards the bus.

We went to the bus conductor. I explained the situation and told him to give her bag from the roof of the bus. He was quick to reply, "I will come with you, but you will have to climb up to take out your own bag." Left with no other option, I had to agree to his terms. So, I climbed the ladder on to the roof of the bus.

"This is a good practice before climbing the mountain," Naira shouted from below. Again, she was beaming at me.

This crazy gorgeous girl was annoying and enchanting at the same time. I honestly didn't know how to react. Whether to laugh at her words or shout back at her. I preferred to stay silent.

When I was halfway up the ladder, I asked her, "Which is your bag?" She replied, "The red bag with the angry bird print," pointing a finger to the right-hand side. 'Ahh...girls and their choices'. It was easy to identify her angry bird massive red duffel bag. I passed it down to her, and stood midway on the ladder. She rummaged through her bag and two minutes later managed to pull out her white and brown flurry jacket. Again I was amused by her choice. Keeping the bag back on the roof top, I climbed down quickly and rushed towards the entrance of the bus.

"Thank you Rihen for helping me...."

I didn't wait to hear the last words, I hurried away from her trying my best to avoid her. She was stomping and running behind me, calling me various names.

Once the bus started, everyone was in a merry mood. Teams formed quickly to play *Antakshari* (A game of the ending letter) and later Dumb-charades. All the participants were singing at the top of their voices, girls were dancing and falling over due to the jerks from the bus. Even Raju Sir couldn't stop himself from joining in the entertainment.

I was content sitting at my window seat, looking out at the dark starry night...into nothingness...

Just then I heard a melodious voice singing my all-time favourite song. I turned around to see who was singing. And lo...it was Naira again. Why does she keep cropping up everywhere? I thought to myself. Naira's sweet-sounding voice rendering one of my favourite love songs brought back memories of someone...

My mind went back into the past...that sweet face, our long conversations, those moments...everything kept coming back to me. I closed my eyes and rested my head on the bus seat. Slowly small drops of tears started trickling down my eyes. But I couldn't let others see them. I wiped them off quickly. Silence engulfed me. I couldn't hear the voice of my fellow trekkers anymore...I was lost in her dreams...her images. The love filled talks, the empty promises, the unfulfilled desires.

I vividly remembered her round face, her ivory coloured skin with rose colour tint on her cheeks. I was attracted towards her mysterious big black eyes, lively and which sparkled with joy when she smiled. When she was sorrowful her eyes seemed to grow dim and dark. This face brought back many memories...many untold stories of the past.

Just then the driver abruptly applied the brakes. I jerked forward and was jolted back to the present. The bus had stopped for a five-minute refreshment break. "This is the last stop for tonight," Raju Sir announced in the bus. "After this we will stop directly in the morning. So, finish all your washroom tasks," he joked. I was the first one to get down, my face still wet and swollen. Everyone else in the bus were still singing and shouting. Trying to hide my tears, I quickly got down and went straight to the washroom. I didn't want anyone to notice my emotions, especially not Sir and not this girl, Naira.

Ten minutes later I was back on my seat, feeling refreshed. Just then others started coming in from the washroom. I plugged in my headphone to listen to songs and closed my eyes. I turned my thoughts to trekking. But instead, my mind wandered back to her thoughts, into the past.

> *Whenever I think of you*
> *It melts my heart.*
> *But at the same time*
> *It tears me apart.*

Out of the blue, Naira came towards my seat. Before I could stop her, she plonked herself on the empty seat beside me. I was aghast at first. A bit embarrassed. I wanted my privacy, and not a noisy, interfering girl sitting next to me. I paused the song on my playlist and took out my headphones.

"Don't you remember me, Rihen?" she asked again innocently.

"Nah...Not really, I can't remember you," I said honestly. I wasn't too keen on a conversation with her. Her closeness made me feel uncomfortable. But I couldn't help noticing her cute dimples. Wearing extra layers of clothes and her flurry jacket with long earrings, she looked funny. Her eyes were looking into my eyes, searching for an answer. I tried to scratch my head trying my best to remember where I had seen this glorious mess that was sitting next to me.

But thankfully she gave the answer to her own question.

"We met a year and a half back at that short trekking trip in Dang. We were in different groups and hardly interacted, but once we had a common task, you were the centre of attraction then, always bubbling with energy, actively participating in the tasks given, very social and friendly with all the fellow trekkers. Don't you remember me? What has happened to you now?"

Now I remembered. On my first trekking trip with friends to the Dang jungle, I had seen Naira. We were a group of 15 trekkers. Naira was one of them. We didn't interact much then, but yes, we had formally met each other in the group. I didn't realise she had noticed so much about me.

I fumbled for words. I didn't know why I should tell this girl about the change in my behaviour. What should I talk to her and why? My mind was racing. Her arms were touching mine, and I was feeling awkward. Her deep innocent eyes were piercing mine, searching for answers. Her soft touch, her pleasant face, her smell...everything was very distracting.

She insisted. "So how are you? What have you been upto in the last year? And why are you so quiet this time?" I still didn't reply. I just shrugged my shoulders.

We sat there in silence for some time.

"I am fine," I finally replied, after a silence of about five minutes. "It's just that I was a bit sick before joining this trip. I'm still getting into the mood for trekking." I tried to evade any further talk. Sensing my discomfort, she also did not question me further. Feeling upset, she went to her seat at the back. I closed my eyes, hid myself into my warm cosy blanket and went off to sleep.

3

The Journey Has Just Begun

The first rays of the morning sun peeped in through the bus window. I opened my eyes and sleepily looked at my watch. It was 6 am. We were in Manali, heading towards the base camp at Prini.

I pushed aside the curtains to look out. And then I partly opened the sliding window of my seat. A breath of fresh air plunged into my nostrils and pushed into my lungs. I felt a sudden vigour of freshness. The view outside was bewitching. The sun was slowly casting its first golden rays on the far majestic Himalayas. The vast blue sky, the snow-covered peaks and the country road was so very captivating. I kept looking out of the window for some time. Once you drive past the traffic along the highways and reach Manali you can feel the air getting fresher, roads going zig-zag and lush greenery everywhere. In Manali, the things you notice are the mountains and the scenery around, uplifting your spirits. It was very cold. I checked the temperature on my mobile. It read 10°c. I wrapped myself in my cosy blanket to keep myself warm.

Someone rightly said that nature can do wonders for you. It had certainly swirled its magic wand on me, for I finally found some peace within myself. I felt happy...and calm, at peace. It was a magical morning. I revelled in my own happiness, in nature's magic for some more time. I was grateful to be alive and present at this moment to witness this beautiful Himalayan landscape in front of me. The scene outside the window presented itself with the most stunning views of nature and its beauty. The Himalayas seemed to come alive during the morning light while the conifers and pine trees carpeted the mountain slopes. From the window of the bus could be seen the jaw-dropping view of brilliant greenery and charming landscape. Nature was at its best today. In that moment, I somehow, forgot all my worries and pain. A sudden calmness engulfed me. I seemed to see things in a different light. I even smiled a bit, after many months.

I looked around. Most of the members were sleeping, some were looking out of their window just like me. Others had plugged in their headphones.

My eyes searched for Naira. On the pretext of taking out something from my bag, I got up from my seat. I took my bag from the overhead rack and started rummaging through it. I glanced at the back seat and saw Naira sleeping peacefully. Her beautiful dimple face looked more beautiful in the morning. The sunlight peered at her through the half-open curtains of her window. This irritated her sleep and she squinted her eyes for a second. Without thinking, I went near her seat and closed the curtains of her window. She now seemed comfortable and was smiling inwardly. Her dimples were very magnetic, making me stare at her face for longer than required. A strand of her thick wavy dark brown hair was titillating her soft pink cheeks. I looked around, no one was watching me. I quietly bent down and put her strand of hair behind her ears very lightly so as not to wake her from the deep sleep. Slowly I moved out from Naira's seat and came back to mine.

Once back at my window, looking out, my thoughts once again trailed back to her...I clearly remembered how she also loved her sleep, how she used to doze off during our incessant chats at night, how she used to keep on twirling her hair with her stubby soft hands. I remembered her long, luscious silky black hair, cute round face, those naughty black eyes, her endless chatter, and our eternal promises. How we used to share all our feelings with each other. Whenever we talked, we always seemed to fall short of time, always eager to meet each other, share things and emotions. We never had to try pleasing each other. There was always warmth, a comfort level already established, then why? Why when I really needed her, she didn't hold on to me? She didn't comfort me. Why did she go away? Why do I miss her so much? Why do I think of her, imagine us together...when I know it's of no use? What is it that attracts me to her? Doesn't she think of me? Am I no longer a priority for her? Lots of confusion...lots of unanswered questions.

Just then I heard a commotion from the back of the bus. Two boys were arguing over something. Everyone had circled around them. I also went at the back to see what the issue was. It turned out that one of the boys named Karan had accidentally tripped over the headphones of the guy sitting across him. The left earplug of the headphone had broken, and the guy who owned the headphones was shouting abuses at Karan.

"You stupid fellow, look what you have done. Couldn't you look down before stepping on top of my headphones?"

Karan yelled back, "It's your fault. You should have kept your headphones safely in your bag after using them. Why did you leave them on the seat so that they fell down?"

"Look, who's talking," the other guy whose name was Rahul started screaming again.

The argument went on for some more time. Even girls crowded around, listening and giggling at the heated discussion. Naira was right there, standing near Karan. She looked very composed and tried to calm down the boys. Naira suggested that Karan should buy new headphones for Rahul from the market in Manali. Rahul readily agreed to this suggestion and at last the fight ended. Rahul settled down in his seat.

"Thank you, Miss for your suggestion", Karan turned towards Naira, and shook her hand with both his hands and held it for a little longer than was necessary. For the first time I noticed how tall and handsome he was.

"No problem, and my name is Naira", she beamed at him.

"Nice to meet you, Naira," Karan smiled.

Then they chatted with each other for some time. I noticed that he was continuously eyeing Naira. He looked handsome, lean and tall in his black track pants hanging loosely around his waist and white shirt sleeves rolled up just above his elbows, the top of his T-shirt unbuttoned. His dark hair was tousled, tossed backwards. He had sharp jaws giving an edgy look to his square face. Overall, Karan looked attractive. Both of them were still talking with each other.

'Why should I bother', I whispered to myself.

Then I saw her coming towards me. "Good morning, Rihen" Naira greeted me with a broad dimpled smile.

"Good morning, Naira," I greeted her back with a smile.

"Wow! you know how to smile also, huh!" she smirked. I casually patted her back. I noticed Karan was looking at us from behind.

Just then Sir shouted from the front, "We will be arriving at our base camp shortly. Girls and boys, pack your bags... get ready. We will reach in about 20 minutes." Everyone in the bus started packing their things. The excitement in the bus was quite visible. Girls were packing and re-packing while laughing all the time. All of us waited with bated breath to reach our base camp. Once the bus stopped and after everyone got down, Raju Sir asked me to check the whole bus for any leftover stuff. I obeyed his command. I checked the bus twice but found nothing. When I stepped out of the bus, the temperature was freezing. Most of the girls were shivering. Boys were acting macho, trying to help the girls carry their luggage and pretending as if they were not feeling cold at all. I had put on two jackets, a woollen hat and warm boots. Along with a few other boys I trailed behind the group to ensure everyone was safe. Raju Sir was at the front, leading the group to our base camp.

We travelled on foot to our Base Camp at Prini, 3-km from Manali. Nestled among the Dhauladhar range, this region is popular amongst trekking groups. Situated amid snow-clad Himalayan peaks and home to picturesque river valleys, green pastures, Prini mesmerized us with its extraordinary scenic beauty. All of us were soaking in nature's endowments. We were awestruck with the view surrounding us. The lush green forests, sprawling meadows carpeted with flowers, gushing blue streams, a rustic mist lingering in the air, and the raw fresh fragrance of pines – Prini, Manali seemed to be like a fairy-tale land.

When we reached our base camp, Sir introduced us to our local trekking guide. Short and stubby, Mr Ching looked a bit funny with bushy eyebrows and small squinted humorous eyes. He reminded me of a funny character in one of the films I had recently seen. Ching Sir seemed to be quite sharp and witty in nature. He greeted us warmly and asked all of us to first settle down into our tents. We did as we were told. He had made all arrangements to ensure a comfortable stay for us in the tents. We were informed beforehand that Mr Ching was a highly experienced Everest summiteer and a knowledgeable instructor. A lady volunteer accompanied him on the camp. There was a team of helpers, support staff and kitchen staff which we were told would look after all our needs during the trekking trip. They were all well trained in First-Aid and Crisis Management. We were introduced one by one to the whole staff.

Then we were shown our tents. There were separate tents for boys and girls. One tent could be shared by 2 or 3 members. There were almost 10 tents arranged symmetrically with a small walkway path dividing the girl's and the boy's tents. A common dustbin was provided between 3-4 tents. There were ropes tied between tents to dry our clothes or hang other things. The toilets were located at the far end of our camp. There were two toilets, one for boys and one for girls. Our tents were surrounded by trees and shrubs. We spotted some horses and mules at the far end corner of our tents. There was a separate big tent for the kitchen, storage and the staff. Overall, the place looked very clean, other than the smelly dirty faeces of the animals littered around the campsite. We could even see the Himalayan range from our base.

We quickly gathered our luggage and moved towards our allotted tents. Ching Sir had randomly placed us together. I was sharing my tent with Lakshya (the boy I had met on the railway platform). I just hoped Lakshya would not bother me with his non-stop blabbering. Karan was in the tent just next to mine. We were taken aback when we saw Rahul also walk up to that tent. Rahul and Karan were sharing the same tent. Oh my gosh! The boys let out a silent cry. Even the girls got anxious. We all hoped that we would not witness any more fights during the next few days.

I went inside our tent. It was huge and spacious from inside and very clean. There was a plastic vinyl sheet covering the bottom of the tent. On it was laid a huge smooth carpet to keep the temperature warm. The tent was waterproof, because the weather in the mountains was very unpredictable. We were provided with sleeping bags, pillows and warm blankets. Lakshya and I chose our sides for sleeping, arranged our luggage and plonked lazily on the sleeping mattress. The day had just begun, there was a lot of excitement, but somehow it was also very tiring. By the time we all had settled down in our tents and freshened up, it was almost 12 pm. Soon we heard a loud gong, a signal to assemble outside for lunch.

"Lunch is ready, everybody please come here," our coach shouted at the top of his voice. In five minutes we all assembled outside on the ground. Everyone was as hungry as a bear. The boys gobbled down their food as if we had not eaten for months. The girls were giggling about something and talking in sign language with each other. Some of the boys were trying hard to seek the attention of these girls and mingle in their group. While having her lunch, Naira glanced at me once or twice and I also smiled back at her. In the backdrop of nature, she looked even more beautiful. I found myself continuously staring at her. She was sitting with her two close friends, who I noticed, had been together since the beginning of the trip. Her chattering, her laugh and her radiant face was so alluring. But I noticed something else. Karan, who was sitting opposite me was also looking fixedly at Naira. I noticed he was trying to divert Naira's attention to himself. But Naira didn't seem interested. Well, it shouldn't matter to me, I whispered to myself and continued with my lunch.

After lunch, we were given some time to rest. Later in the afternoon, we were told that Ching Sir would be briefing us about our trekking trip. Being tired from the long bus journey and the walk to the base camp, most of the members went into their tents to rest. Some of the girls gathered in one tent and were playing games. I didn't rest and instead planned to go to the market to get some alcohol. I had been for trekking before and knew very well that the cold temperature here could be bearable only with rum. I knew this would be needed on the journey. It was too cold here and I thought it best to stock up on some rum bottles. I went to Raju Sir and quietly asked for his permission. Of course, it is not allowed legally, so Raju Sir asked me to be very careful and bring the alcohol quietly without making a furore. He gave me strict instructions to keep this a secret but also guided me to the shop from which to buy and how to bargain. I agreed and went quietly out of the base camp without making any noise or informing anyone else.

I took a bus from the main road near our base camp to go to Mall Road, Manali. Situated on a hill overlooking the splendid Kullu Valley, Mall Road was lined with multiple hotels, restaurants and bars. There were plenty of shops and emporiums too. From the local Kullu and Kashmiri shawls, rugs, woollen caps, jewellery to wooden furniture and books, the Mall Road offered a lot of options for shoppers. There was a network of by-lanes from the main road with smaller shopping zones. I had read somewhere that these were also referred to as the 'heart of the town', hence Mall Road was always buzzing with local crowd and tourists. Luckily the area was not as crowded as it was afternoon. I roamed around the marketplace for a while before heading to the wine shop in a dingy corner of the lonely street. Furnished with old, dusty wooden interiors, this was a small wine shop with a cosy restaurant at the back. Pop music of the 90s was playing in the background. I ordered two small bottles of rum and one bottle of whiskey. The man behind the counter indulged in small chit chat with me. I bought the bottles, thanked him and came out of the shop.

The cold temperature was affecting my appetite as well. I realised that I was hungry, so I went to a local eatery and ordered hot vegetable curry and Momos. Later, I strolled around on the shopping street. I bought myself a pair of black gloves as I had forgotten to bring them. I also bought a warm maroon shawl with beautiful Kashmiri embroidery for my mother from one of the handloom shops, a bright yellow floral print scarf for my sister and Himachal traditional cap for my dad.

I looked at my watch. It was 3 pm. I had to reach the camp on time for the briefing which was to start at 3.30 pm.

Knowing I couldn't carry much luggage during trekking, I resisted any more shopping and finally took a bus to our base camp. Back at the camp, I went quietly inside. From the corner of my eyes, I saw Raju Sir glancing in my direction. I winked at him, indicating the bag in my hand. He gave me a nod. I went into my tent and hid the rum bottles inside my back pack. I was right on time as just then the gong for our afternoon tea rang and everyone started coming out of their tents. I heaved a sigh of relief and got ready for the briefing.

4

'Trekking' – Experience of a Lifetime

All the participants assembled outside for tea. I joined the others. We were served tea, coffee and some biscuits.

"All of you hurry up and have your tea and coffee, for we will be starting the briefing in 15 minutes," Raju Sir announced.

At exactly 3.30 pm, Ching Sir started our briefing. All of us stood in a big circle facing each other. Naira was standing opposite me. I saw Karan was standing next to her. Was it a coincidence or did he purposely go and stand next to her? And why was I thinking so much about them? Ching Sir was strolling around the group, giving out instructions while walking. Raju Sir and the other support staff were standing at the right-hand corner of the circle.

First, we were all given a warm welcome, followed by an ice-breaking session to introduce all the participants to each other and to the trekking staff. Next, he gave us a brief insight into our upcoming trekking journey. We were given general instructions on our behaviour and how to conduct ourselves during the trek. We were informed about the equipment which we would need and the rules that we had to follow.

Ching Sir began the talk, "Sour Tal Lake is one of the most spectacular and scenic high-altitude trek in the Kullu valley. It is one of the few trek which has not yet been fully explored, starting from this Prini Base Camp, the trek winds through the Dhauladhar range through lush green valleys, high-altitude meadows and dazzling landscapes. To keep you company, are the peaks of the Pir-Panjal range. Our trek will leave Manali valley, proceed further through the evergreen forests of Cedar, Silver Fir, Walnut, Oak and the Silver Birch. We have to pass through Klount to finally reach Sour Tal Lake. You must have already gone through the itinerary provided beforehand. Keep it handy, along with a map of this region in your backpack. It will always be useful."

The activities covered during the Trek will include:

* Camping
* Trekking
* Basic Rock Climbing
* Rappelling
* River Crossing
* Net Climbing
* River Rafting

The following trekking instructions were given in brief:

* Hot water and bath facilities are at your disposal only at the base camp. Once you leave the base camp,

there will be no bath water or hot water available for anyone.

- Electricity and other basic facilities are available at base camp only. As you go up there is no electricity. You will all have to use a torch. Phones are to be charged at the base camp. As you climb, you will have to use your power banks.
- While trekking, don't use headphones as you will not be able to hear any emergency shout, or noise from a nearby wild animal. Always stay alert of your surroundings, and be watchful of any peculiar activity.
- Don't litter your surroundings. Put waste in your bag. There will be a ditch at every camp. You will throw garbage only in that ditch so that later we can burn it and put mud on it.
- While trekking, all the participants are requested to follow the rule of maintaining 2-3 feet distance between two trekkers.
- Leave your main luggage and everything else down at the base camp. Pack only necessities in your rucksack. Take all the essentials as you cannot come back to base camp in case you forget anything.
- Carry only those things which you might need while trekking. Don't burden yourself with unnecessary things and increase your load. Carry only basic essentials like bottle of water, mobile, camera if you have, poncho (type of a raincoat), and wind cheater. In case there is more baggage, we do have a facility to rent mules and porters to carry your luggage to the given points. However, you will have to pay from your own pockets for the extra facilities that you avail.

- Every day as we go higher, the camp sites will change. And every day there will be a different activity to do. Everyone has to actively participate in all the activities unless they have a valid reason for not participating.
- In special cases of poor health condition, the participants will not be allowed to continue the trek. They will be sent back to this base camp and will be taken care of and looked after by the locals.
- Every participant will follow the rules and maintain discipline, otherwise you will be punished.

After this we were given instructions on the LNT practices followed by a group discussion on the same.

LNT stands for Leave No Trace Principles - simply put, it's the best practices that participants of a trekking camp have to follow to enjoy and protect our natural resources.

The Leave No Trace Principles

1. *Plan ahead and prepare:* This includes doing research about your destination and packing appropriately.
2. *Travel and camp on durable surfaces:* Ideal durable surfaces include established trails and campsites, rock, gravel, dry grasses or snow.
3. *Dispose waste properly:* This applies to everything from litter to human waste to rinse water. Keep the surroundings clean before you leave a place.
4. *Minimize campfire impacts (be careful with fire):* Use a lightweight stove for cooking and put out campfires completely before leaving a site.

5. *Leave what you find:* Examine, but do not touch cultural or historic structures and artefacts. Leave rocks, plants and other natural objects as you find them.
6. *Respect wildlife:* Observe wildlife from a distance. Do not follow or approach them.
7. *Be considerate of other visitors:* Be courteous to other users on the trail.

"Is everything clear?" Ching Sir shouted at the top of his voice.

"Yes", we all replied in unison.

"Good. So, enjoy and take it easy for today. However, we will do a trial acclimatisation walk. From tomorrow, you will have to wake up early. We will start our trek early in the morning and then go to our next base camp."

"Ok Sir," we all answered back loudly.

Later, a few girls had some doubts over sanitary hygiene and stuff like that which they cleared with the lady volunteer.

Before finally wrapping up the meeting, Ching Sir told us in a serious tone, "Many of you are first-time trekkers. Most of you are amateurs. You may feel nervous about the challenge ahead, of trekking through the daunting mountains. Trekking is not as easy as you think. And certainly not fun. It is more of an exercise for your body and soul. It is normal to feel anxious, to back out during the tedious tasks and the hard climb. But remember one thing- at the end of all this, you'll come out with an experience of a lifetime. To live amongst nature, to feel its beauty is magical. Yet be ready for unforeseen surprises from nature. There will be no basic facilities which you all are so used to in your daily life in the city. Washrooms may not be always available and you may need to go out in the woods. Drinking water is not filtered here and hence, get accustomed to drinking boiled or upstream water. Brace yourselves for a mixed bag of experience, where you will have to come out of your comfort zone and gel with nature and its resources. Proper toilets, bathing, mineral water, electricity, mobile charging, network are all luxuries which you need to forget as long as you are here. But these surreal experiences will ultimately leave a magical feeling in your heart and mind forever! memories that will linger with you throughout your life."

"So, participants quickly get ready for your trial trek. We are leaving in 15 minutes for an acclimatization walk up to Arjun Gufa, Sharvani Devi Temple and Thakshak Nag Bhanara. This area, an oasis of green flanked by the densely forested hills surrounding it, is just a short walk from our campsite. It is just a trial walk and we will be back at the camp within a few hours. Come on now group, get going," Ching Sir shouted cheerfully.

With this, he ended his hour-long briefing. We held on to the few words he had said about this being an experience of a lifetime. It filled us with renewed zest and energy for the upcoming trip. We were already spellbound by the beauty of nature and knew this was definitely going to be a memorable experience of a lifetime!

All of us scrambled back to our tents to quickly get our rucksacks ready with just the essentials. Lakshya and I put on our tracks, T-shirt, a wind-cheater and trekking boots.

Both of us got ready in a jiffy. We were the first ones out. Soon some other guys and girls joined us. Last to join the group were Naira and her friends. Ching Sir wasn't happy about it.

"Sorry, we are late," Naira pleaded with Sir.

"Please excuse her Sir, this is the first time," Karan was clearly supporting her.

Naira and I, both looked at him in surprise. He didn't even know her properly, yet he was continuously seen around Naira and taking her side. I was amazed why it was bothering me.

"Since this is a trial trek, it is okay for now. I am ignoring your late coming. But from tomorrow if you are not on time, you will be punished," Ching Sir told her sternly.

Naira clearly looked upset. "Very well Sir, I will make sure to be punctual," she replied innocently.

We started our trial trek by late afternoon. Ching Sir was leading the group. We all trailed behind him in a single line keeping 2-feet distance between us, as per the rules. One support staff was walking in the middle while Raju Sir tagged along at the end of the group to keep a watch on everyone ahead.

We trailed through splendid summer pastures, along flocks of sheep and their shepherds and fascinating pathways. Soon we came to a small narrow single road surrounded on both sides by the homes of the locals. Most of the houses had traditional stone slate roofs. Some of them had old wooden structures. Many children came out seeing a big group like ours. We all were captivated by the beauty and cuteness of these children. Their innocent little bright faces, their cheeks glowing red with a broad smile on their pink lips, their golden-brown curls shone in the melting sunshine. They shook hands with us and looked pleased to see us all. But we were double happy seeing such cute faces. It made our day. Many of us took photographs with these children. The girls were more gaga over them, clicking pictures, laughing and mingling with these little bundles of joy. Many of the locals also came out seeing all the excitement and the hullabaloo. The local people seemed so simple, and yet so beautiful.

We moved on along our trail towards the Temple. A few minutes later, while taking a steep turn, I saw a girl struggling with her rucksack, unable to handle it. She was three participants ahead of me. Her friends tried to help her but they couldn't manage being burdened with their own heavy bags. She stopped over to handle the bag and 'Splash...' her right foot slipped into a dung of horse poop. 'Eeee yuck', I heard her yelling. While walking, I reached where she had stopped. She was still trying to clear out of the mess she was in.

"May I help you with the bag?" I asked.

She looked up and beamed a huge smile, "Of course Rihen, you are too good in helping with my luggage. Please help me out of this mess," she said while trying to brush off the poop from her shoes with a stick.

'Aah, it turned out to be Naira. My concern for the girl vanished quickly.' I lifted her bag and it was damn heavy.

"Naira are you carrying stones or what in your bag?"
I quizzed her.

"'Oh, just some necessary things Rihen," pat came her
reply.

"You seem to have a lot of necessary things," I smirked
at her. "For now, just take out a few things from your bag
and put them in mine. And next time travel light," I told her.

She wiped her hands and feet with wet tissues and then
quickly emptied some of her things into my bag.

"What's going on?" we heard Raju Sir coming towards us
from behind. "Sir, I am just trying to help Naira with her
luggage." I winked at him.

"Ok, carry on with the trek," saying this Sir went back
to the end of the group.

After about two hours of uphill walk, we reached our
destination Bhanara, situated at a height of 2200m. Here
there was an old temple dedicated to the local God Takshak
Nag. The Takshak Nag temple is adorned by decorative
wood carvings. We all went inside the temple. While I joined
my hands to pray, I looked around. My eyes fell upon
Naira. Her beauty captured me. The long wavy hair now
tied in a ponytail, her blush dimpled cheeks, and her rosy
lips bewitched my senses. She was praying with her head
down and her eyes closed. She looked as innocent as a dove
at that moment. I was still staring at her when she opened
her eyes and suddenly looked in my direction. I turned my
face in the opposite side, away from her glare. To avoid
her confrontation, I quickly went out with some boys and
decided to stay with them before she could catch me.

After resting at the temple, our group marched ahead. Near Bhanara, there were the remnants of a fort of Raja Piti, an earlier ruler of Kullu. Near the fort is the historic cave (Arjun Gufa) where Arjun of Mahabharata is believed to have taken refuge during the exile of the Pandavas. We examined the cave. It was dark and frightening inside. Some of the participants became claustrophobic and immediately went outside. Lakshya, Karan, me and some other boys were still inside the cave along with Ching Sir. We found the caves quite intriguing and were enjoying making weird echoes. Lakshya was too fascinated and was playing hide and seek in the darkness of the ancient rustic caves. We reached a focal point, a dark deep chamber where Ching Sir asked us to lay down on the floor and close our eyes for five minutes. We did as we were told. After five minutes, when we opened our eyes and looked up on the ceiling, we could see a labyrinth of towers, roads and lanes. It looked as if we were staring at a busy street of some metropolitan city. Such was the effect of the ceiling of the cave. We gasped in astonishment. After spending a considerable amount of time in the caves we came out.

Many participants were resting. Sitting on rocks and boulders, people were catching their breath. Just then Raju Sir announced that since it was getting dark and we were tired, our bus would take us back to our base camp. On hearing this, we heaved a sigh of relief! Though it was an easy trek, being the first day we were exhausted and hungry. All of us being very tired, we thanked Sir for taking us back in the bus rather than walking the entire way. During our journey back to the camp, there was pin-drop silence in the bus. No one talked or laughed or even joked.

We reached base camp by 8 pm. Dinner was ready. As soon as we approached the camp, hot aroma of spicy vegetable curry and sweet smell of rice filled our noses. We all were so hungry that we just washed our hands and sat down for dinner. We all gobbled up the food as if we had not eaten for 2-3 days. After dinner, there wasn't much energy left in any of us to do anything. Most of us went off to sleep knowing we had an early morning start the next day.

5

Change in Behaviour

O ur second day at the camp began at 6.00 am. Poetic birdcalls and warm sunlight ensured we woke up early. There was a long queue at the washrooms. Some couldn't control their nature's call and went off into the woods. We had to bathe with cold water, which gave us goose bumps. I was waiting for my turn at the boy's bathroom and could hear a loud hoarse voice singing a famous Shahrukh Khan Song from inside. From the top open window we could see his arms in the air swaying in tune with the song. It was so hilarious that we all were laughing while waiting outside. Since most of us couldn't take the freezing water for long, we all freshened up very quickly.

By 7.00 am we were sipping hot cups of mint tea. It was cold and most of us were packed with two-three layers of clothing. There was a lot of chattering and excitement amongst the group. After all our actual trek was to begin today. Tea was followed by a small warm-up session.

We were given a brief about the day's trek by Ching Sir.

"The trek will start from here Prini down to Bhanu Bridge and over the Beas River to the other side of the valley. We will follow a gradual climb up to Gadherini village and after that the steep section starts along the cedar trees right up to Klount. The trek encompasses an hour of steep ascent initially and then turns into a zigzag way till Klount through dense forest of Blue Pine, Cedar, Oak, Silver Fir. Klount is situated in the middle of a dense forest, located amidst Apple orchards on the mountain. a fertile and grassy land where herds of sheep were kept in the olden days. We will have adventure activities in the evening and then stay overnight at Klount. In short, our trail would ascend through forest of pines and cedars till the Hilly Base Camp, which is a 4-hours trek."

"Understood everyone?" Sir asked us.

"Yes Sir," we all said quite feebly for our voices were blocked by the cold.

"Oh, and I forgot to tell you this...." Ching Sir started giving instructions again.

"I would like to give a small piece of advice to all the trekkers. You should always carry basic medicines, Band-Aids, rain cover, hats, sun glasses, trekking stick, insect repellent, towels and toilet paper which can be quite handy. It is also recommended that you carry water purification tablets. There are tiny stalls along the way that sell noodles and tea for short stopovers and even offer boiled water. But it is advisable to be on the safe side and carry your own. We should consider ourselves lucky since our trekking group has employed a local cook to provide breakfast, lunch on the go and dinner. Also, it is our primary duty to take all the necessary precautions to avoid forest fire."

"Any questions?" he asked us again.

"No Sir," this time the reply was loud and clear.

After a quick but hearty breakfast, all trekkers along with Ching Sir and Raju Sir assembled at the starting point. We all had our backpacks, walking sticks and we started towards Bhanu Bridge. Along with us was a pack of mules loaded with kitchen utensils and raw supplies for cooking. We carried our small backpacks with just the essentials, while all our large backpacks and some extra luggage was laden on the mules. We were handed our "energy packs" for the day – tetra pack fruit juice and a bar of nuts and chocolate. After exchanging goodbyes and good luck wishes we all set off!

So here we were on our way to the second base camp on the second day of the trek, as we toiled up, step after step. We moved in a single line with Ching Sir in front, as usual, and Raju Sir bringing up the rear. The staff and cook were walking along with the mules. We were mesmerised by the fabulous view of the snow-capped mountains and lavish greenery which met our eyes at the first halt at Bhanu Bridge. The sound of the crystal clear Beas River gushing in green and blue swirls across boulders and gorges under the bridge was quite loud. We were happy to have a 15-minutes stop. Most of us got busy in taking pictures of the beautiful scenery before us.

Lakshya and I stood at the far end of the bridge. The girls stopped in the middle of the bridge. I could see some girls joking aloud. They were posing for a picture at the edge of the bridge. And the picture was being taken by none other than Karan. He looked like a pro with his advanced DSLR camera and shooting techniques. He seemed to be thoroughly enjoying this female attention. He started training some of the girls on how to pose in different angles as if doing a modelling shoot. When he showed the pictures to the group of girls, they all screamed in delight. They were very happy and thanked Karan again and again. I chuckled at his popularity, wondering if the pictures he took were really that great or he was just fooling around with the girls. I noticed Naira also observing everything. I gave her a faint smile. She waved back at me.

Soon, our group resumed the trek, but we were not in any hurry. We crossed the bridge and started the climb for the mountain valley on the other side. At a height of 2,680mts, Gadherini village was a few kilometres from there. The road was uneven, with large boulders and surrounded by tall conifers and pines. Little wonder, city dwellers like us were soon panting like motor engines at full steam. Even though I had been to a trek earlier, I still felt drained halfway through. The upper body was still fine, but our thighs were protesting. This was the case with most of us. Many of them stopped, bending over their knees, some stretched themselves while others took sips of water. I took out my energy bar and finished it off in one go. In fact, the girls appeared to be stronger than the boys, for they kept on moving while boys were taking breaks in between. Stopping to look around us was one of the ways in which we could let our body regain control of itself. Once on top of the mountain looking down into the valley, the panoramic view, the blue sky and the fresh air were just breath-taking. The valley rose in layers from the plains to encompass the mountainous terrain, high-altitude meadows and plateaus.

I was told by the porters who were driving the mules and carrying our bags that the sky was expected to change its mood by early afternoon and it might also rain. They said the weather in the hills was very unpredictable. We carried on, up and up, still higher, across hillsides and past meadows that invited us to linger but we couldn't do so. The air was laced with the sound of bells as the mules trudged past us.

We reached Gadherini village by afternoon, where we halted for our lunch. A walk down to the village showed us a typical Himachal village. Gadheriniwas a good drop below Klount, a bustling village complete with a temple and some local shops. There were a few houses of the local *'pahadis'* (People living in the hills), their roofs glinting in the sun. Far from the maddening city crowd, it was good to meet and interact with the simple locals. Women clad in their traditional dresses were sitting out, pounding grain, some busy with embroidery work. There was a constant buzz of activity with women talking to each other, cute red-faced children playing and running here and there. The men were out working in the fields or in the shops and some even went to the city for work. We also had the company of some little hens and chicks. The vibrant natural atmosphere of the village cheered our moods. All the tiredness seemed to drift away. We all were enjoying the company of the local people.

Lunch was modest with rice and vegetable curry. We were instructed to go to a nearby stream to drink water. Some of us carried bottled water in our backpacks, which we had filled from the base site. Some of us, including me, drank the bottled water. I saw Naira and her friends, Karan and his friends and the group of girls whose pictures he had clicked go to the stream ahead to drink water. Suddenly a bunch of children ran towards Karan squeaking like a hawk, demanding him to take their photos. Karan, who was at that time taking photos of the scenery, obliged the kids. He turned his DSLR camera towards the kids and started taking pictures of the adorable cheeky children. He even shot some amazing videos, from what I heard. The group of girls also posed with them. Just then I saw Naira approach him. They were talking about something. Naira seemed to be requesting Karan for something. Karan looked very pleased at that moment, quite happy with himself. The next moment Karan was taking Naira's picture with the children. He held her hand to show her the poses and took quite a few photos. Naira looked very happy and Karan had a broad smile on his handsome face.

After bidding the children goodbye, Karan and Naira went near the gurgling stream, where he took three-four more photos of Naira with her friends. She also gave different poses, smiling and giggling at him as he happily took her pictures. I was watching all this from a distance. I don't know why I was interested in what Karan or Naira doing. It shouldn't have bothered me, but it did.

"Karan takes amazing pictures. He is actually a professional photographer. That's why everyone is requesting him to click their pictures."Lakshya who had come by my side informed me.

"Huh, oh nice," I replied, surprised by the small piece of information given by Lakshya.

"And his short videos are even more awe-inspiring. You should see how skilfully he shoots the videos of our trek. Everyone is praising his photography skills. And now, he has got a lot of female fans as well," Lakshya passed on some more information.

'No wonder!' I muttered to myself casually. Naira seems to be his latest fan, I thought to myself.

"It's time to proceed now," we heard Ching Sir's loud voice. The short break had restored our energy.

We continued through the mountains. After a hair-raising walk through the tracks, we gradually moved upslope. There was a new level of excitement visible across the group. I guess nature and the delicious food had upped our spirits. Suddenly, out of now here, Naira appeared behind me. She and her friends walked past us. She was just two members ahead of me. We all walked at a fast pace, eager to reach our next destination. The trek was long, but we went along singing and humming, sometimes listening to the melodious tunes of the birds in the woods. The tall pines whispered in the wind, boulders suddenly appeared along the narrow path and the vegetation was still fresh but different. I had my eyes on Naira most of the time. And she often looked back at me on one pretext or the other. After a pleasant one hour's walk we finally made it to our Camp at Klount (2,230mts). Klount, located in the mountain enclaves amidst the depths of the forest and vast apple orchards, was a sight to behold. Rich forests of silver fir, blue pine and cedar surrounded the mountainside. The majestic mountain range looked even more awesome from the tent site. Living among nature had never been more beautiful.

Our luggage had already arrived with the mules and we were quickly assigned our tents by Ching Sir. The tents at Klount were basic. Wooden cots lined the walls and there were piles of rough quilts filled with soft wool. Though we were irritated with the army of insects buzzing around us, the scenery was just mesmerizing. Fortunately, a few girls had brought extra insect repellents and we used it liberally to cover our arms and legs. We were four boys in a tent this time. One of them immediately lit a mosquito repellent stick to keep away the insects. Nevertheless, staying in the tents was the best way to experience the untamed surroundings. Lakshya never seemed to leave my side as he was again put in my tent. Maybe he was meant to accompany me till the last day of the trip. We were very tired after the half day's trek. Most of us took a nap, after settling down in our respective tents.

Later in the day, a message was passed down to us that from tomorrow there won't be any way to charge our phones. So, we were asked to do so at this camp here. We were provided with power sockets to charge our phones, music players and power banks whatever. There was a mad rush amongst the group to charge their equipment. Everyone wanted to be the first to use the charger. We were also told to call our parents or loved ones today itself as there won't be any network available. Those who were awake, quickly took out their phones and called their dear ones. We had to come out of our tents to make a call. Outside, there were at least 10 trekkers moving around haphazardly in different directions, each talking on their mobile. I chose a quiet corner, far from everyone and dialled my Mom's number.

"Hi Rihen, how are you son? How's your trip so far?" said a gentle loving voice on the other side of the line.

"Hi Mom. I am fine. How are you, Dad and Nisha?"I got a bit emotional.

"We are all fine beta," Mom replied.

"I tried calling Nisha several times but she did not answer my call," I told her.

"Yes, she has gone to her friend's house since yesterday to study. I will tell her you called. How's the weather there? Put on your jacket and woollen clothes if it's too cold. And are you eating properly? How is the food? Is it tasty and healthy? Please take care of yourself," my mother sounded very anxious over the phone.

"I am fine Mom. Missing you and Nisha alot. And, this is not my first trekking trip. So don't worry. And yeah, we will be trekking higher tomorrow. There will be no network up there. So, now for three days I won't be able to call. You take care and say hi to everyone. Ok bye," with this I ended my phone call.

When I turned back, Naira was standing right behind me. I don't know what got into me, but I got angry seeing her standing like that, eavesdropping on my personal conversation.

"So, you were listening to my phone call, huh?" I questioned her in an irritating tone. "Why are you always lurking around me and hearing my personal conversations?" I was quite annoyed with her and showed her my anger.

Instead of answering my questions, Naira questioned back. "Rihen, why are you behaving in this way? What is wrong with you? Last time you were enjoying yourself so much in the camp that you never missed your family and didn't even bother to talk properly with them. This time you are behaving in a weird manner in the camp, but are talking in a nice and caring way with your Mom. How can someone change so much?" she was staring at my face, the delicate lips twirling in confusion, her eyebrows frowning and her arms folded, waiting for my answer.

I was in no mood to give her any answers. "Why are you noticing so much about me? Leave me alone. Please go away from me," I said nastily.

Hearing this her face dropped. I saw her eyes turning red not knowing whether it was due to tears or rage. The anger in her eyes showed the concern she felt for me. I could see she was really upset with me. I was aware that I had hurt her, but I couldn't help her in anyway. I didn't talk to her. I didn't calm down her anger. It was all too much for me to handle. The care, the concern, her anger, her frustration...I just let her be the way she was...I couldn't help it, it's just how I felt at that time. I was too mad at her to apologise for my behaviour or rectify it at that moment. As she stormed away, I glanced at her face which was still blazing under her stony expression. I didn't care much about it and went towards my tent.

In the evening, we were introduced to various rock-climbing gear and equipment followed by a practical session on the rocks. Ching Sir taught us various kinds of knot-tying and climbing techniques. After the long trek, this exercise was tiring and enjoyable at the same time. Our legs seemed to be giving in while practising. Later we were divided into teams and allotted rock-climbing tasks. Karan, Naira and one of her friends were in the same team. For the first time, to my surprise, Lakshya instead of being my partner was also in their team. I was paired with some other group members in the second team. I looked at Naira. This time she didn't smile at me. In fact, she looked as if she was still furious with me. Behind the fake dimpled smile that she wore on her face, I could sense a feeling of sadness and anger. Even Karan must have noticed her grumpy mood, for he constantly tried to make her smile. I knew it was my fault, but I was just not brave enough to apologise to her.

When Ching Sir blew the whistle, we carried out our allotted tasks. I climbed the rock easily, due to my previous experience. Then I helped my team members with their tasks. In the opposite team, Lakshya found it difficult to even tie a rope knot. Some other members in Karan's team could hardly manage to climb the rock. At the end of our competition, our team had won the rock-climbing task.

After a whole day of hard work, we all lazed around in our tents till dinner time. We were all very hungry and gobbled the hot delicious *masala khichdi* and *kadhi* which was served with salad and *papad*. I don't know why but my eyes were automatically searching for Naira. I saw her standing quietly in a corner with her dinner plate, scraping her spoon in an almost empty dish. Her face showed signs of sadness. When she was alone, I went up to her.

Before I could say anything, she turned to me and asked, "Why have you come here, Mr Rude?" (So she had given me a new name now)

"Look, I am sorry," I told her quietly.
    "Oh, so there is a word 'sorry' also in the dictionary of Mr Rude, huh!" she replied sarcastically.
    "I think it's the only word that can change your current mood," I replied softly.
    "And why is someone noticing my mood?" Naira retorted.
    "I am not observing any such thing, don't create more confusion," I told her.
    "Oh, I see," saying this she went away from me and joined her friends.

Not knowing what to do, I also went towards my tent.

Post dinner, our tent was filled with clothes lying here and there. But no one bothered to tidy it. We were all engrossed in our own fun. The three of us were laughing as Lakshya kept us entertained with his mimicry of various artists. A few girls from the next tent joined us. I peeked outside our tent in case I could spot Naira and call her to join us. However, there was no sign of her. The lights of most of the other tents were off. But in our tent, we all had a lot of fun.

6

The Cozy Night

It was 12.15 at night. I was unable to sleep. A whirlpool of thoughts kept running in my mind. I picked up my phone and went to the last dialled number, my mom's name displayed on the screen. I rang my mother but instantly cut off the call. I couldn't disturb her so late at night. She must be fast asleep. Even Lakshya was snoring loudly on the opposite bed. He was all snuggled up in two huge blankets. His snores were too irritating. The other two members were sleeping peacefully amidst his snores. I took my phone and went out of the tent. I sat near a small bonfire lit by the staff members. It was really cold. I closely wrapped the blanket I had brought with me. Glancing around to make sure that no one was watching, I quietly took out my rum bottle. The cold wind was hitting hard at my weary face. I quickly gulped down two-thirds of the bottle in one go. Aah…I started feeling nice and warm now. There was pin-drop silence, except the buzzing of the night insects. The mules were also fast asleep. Far away I could see some lights in the valley. Must be the locals, I thought to myself.

I lay down on the bare ground with my head resting on my small rucksack. The rustic smell of the earth was very soothing. I looked around once more to make sure no one was awake or hidden in the bushes watching me and then I took a sip or two more of the rum. My head felt a bit dizzy. I thought of all the things that had happened since yesterday. So far, the trip had been good. Since this was my second trekking trip, I was comfortable with the long walking hours, the thrilling activities and all the necessary precautions that had to be taken. Unlike others, who had started complaining about the lack of facilities for bathing and toilet, I was used to them.

I looked up at the sky. The stars shimmering like diamonds, seemed to be within an arm's reach in the pitch-black sky. I moved my hand in a pattern, trying to make out the various constellations in the luminous maze. Then I sat up and did a bottoms-up of the rum. For a moment, I felt I was in some other world, a supernatural space of my own. The stellar sky seemed like a huge celestial canvas, with the gigantic mountains forming the backdrop.

The rum seemed to be having its effect because I got lost into a dreamy world...

We were dancing under the shinning moonlight near the edge of the valley. She was looking like a princess in her ivory-coloured satin and lace gown. Her long tresses were tied beautifully into a French plait. She had put one arm on my shoulder and the other on my waist. I was wearing a blue three-piece suit with sleek shiny shoes. We twirled and swirled to the beats of the soft music, looking into each other's eyes, romancing under the bright moonlight. I kissed her forehead lightly and she smiled. Slowly our lips curved and found each other. She caressed my lips and so did I until we lost all senses and indulged in a deep passionate kiss. I embraced her gently into my arms. She rested her head on my chest...I held her tightly, not wanting to let go.

When I opened my eyes, I saw a distant figure, clad fully in white. The night was dark and eerily silent with not a sound of the chilly wind or the birds in the trees. There was pin-drop silence. Just then I heard a raspy voice, "What are you doing here?" Startled, I turned around and was petrified to see a ghostly figure standing a short distance behind me. Wearing a furry hat over open long hair, a full-length white woollen robe, the figure looked like a ghost straight from a horror movie. I let out a frightened cry. In the darkness, the hooded figure scared me. The silence of the night was scaring me further. I tried to keep still. But my cold body shivered, more from the figure standing there rather than the cold temperature.

Despite the chilled wind, there were drops of perspiration on my forehead. I knew about the many ghost stories, about those who were lost in the mountains and now wandered around, targeting such trekking camps. I tried to look around in the hope that someone might be awake. I wiped the drops of sweat from my forehead and turned to gaze back at the sky. I folded my hands and kept on fidgeting with my fingers. I closed my eyes to pray to God. Only you can save me lord. And then she pinched me hard on my arm, "Hey, it's me, Naira" she said.

I opened my eyes and looked closely at the figure standing before me. She was laughing hilariously at me.

"Ohhhh! Naira, Oh my God! You scared the hell out of me," I said annoyingly, my arms still trembling. "What are you doing out here at this time of the night, you stupid girl?" I was still angry at her for scaring me like this.

She looked at me with a puzzled face. Frowning, the cute dimpled smile vanished from her half-sleepy face. "I should be the one asking you this question," she said sarcastically. "What are you doing here, sitting all alone past midnight? Huh?" She questioned me and stood there waiting for my answer.

"I'm just chilling", I tried to laugh it off.

"It's not funny Rihen," she scowled at me.

"Okay, I wasn't feeling sleepy and came out here to enjoy the night view. "What about you?" I asked her.

The ghostly figure that had frightened me earlier was now replaced by a dainty little girl. The light from the moon illuminated her face like an angel. I was captivated by this shinning white silhouette.

"Even I wasn't feeling sleepy. Then I started feeling very cold and was looking for my shawl in the tent. After searching for about 10 minutes, I realised I had actually left it somewhere around here after dinner. So, I came to collect it," she explained.

She looked around for her shawl and finally found it near one of the tents. She picked it up, wrapped it around her delicate body and came and sat next to me. It seemed as if she didn't want to miss a chance to be with me and talk to me. I thought she might still be upset with me for what had happened in the afternoon. But her anger had disappeared and she appeared quite normal.

"So..." she said.
"So....?" I asked.

"Tell me..." she looked right into my brown eyes. I dared not blink. Her eyes looked into mine as if searching for some answers. Mine were trying not to show the hidden emotions.

> The deep creases on your forehead
> The dark circles beneath your eyes
> Tell the story of a man
> Hiding sadness beneath his smile
> I have never seen a more sorrowful face
> Your pain is what I wish to embrace!

She took a deep breath, came closer and whispered in my ears, "What is wrong with you Rihen? Why are you behaving this way? I might not be able to solve your problems but sharing them will definitely make you feel better. I know enough to understand when you're fine and when you're not and I think I have a right to know what happened."

I was taken aback by her accurate observation of my behaviour. How could a girl with whom I had hardly interacted know so much about me? How could she guess that something was wrong with me? I wondered to myself.

She shook my shoulders, trying to bring me out of my reverie. "Rihen, Rihen...what is wrong with you? Answer me." She had a pleading look on her face, her eyes almost bulging out and her lips continuously speaking my name. I didn't wish to reply or give her any explanation about my situation. I got up and started going back to my tent. The very last thing I wished for was a fight with Naira. I tried to avoid confronting her. But I guess I failed in my attempts. She stood in my way with her open hands. "You are not going anywhere Mr Rihen, before you answer my questions."

"And why should I answer to you?" saying this I shrugged off her hands and moved past her towards my tent.

Without looking at her, I hastily took off from the scene and rushed towards my tent. But the next moment... crassshhh...I bumped into Karan. 'Oh no'...I mumbled...not him.

"Hey, hey, watch out buddy," Karan squealed.
    "Uh oh, hey Karan, I'm sorry." I apologised to him. "By the way, what are you doing out here?"

The night which had seemed quiet and peaceful a while ago, suddenly turned into a nightmare with people coming and disturbing my solitude. First Naira and now Karan. I was very irritated.

Karan took out a small packet of cigarettes from his track pants pocket and winked at me. I signalled to him to where Naira was standing, trying to caution him to smoke discreetly. He slithered the cigarette pack back into his pocket. Then he put his arm around my shoulder and dragged me back to where Naira was standing alone.

"Where are you taking me buddy? I want to go sleep," I said to Karan.

"Only 10 minutes buddy," saying this Karan dragged me along with him towards Naira.

"Hey Naira, not feeling sleepy?" Karan asked her.

I was feeling uncomfortable standing there with the two of them. I didn't dare look directly at Naira. Instead, I looked around, trying to hide my discomfort.

"Yes Karan, I was unable to sleep. Why don't you come along and give me company? It's a beautiful night," saying this she pulled him along with her and totally ignored me. I was taken aback by her abrupt behaviour. A few minutes ago she was talking to me, wanting to know the reason behind my behaviour. Now she was acting so normal and wished for Karan to give her company. 'Uff...these girls', by thinking this I started to walk away from them. But then my ego was hurt. How could she ignore me like this? That too in front of another guy? I cared less about Karan and went back to join them both. Karan was surprised by my sudden appearance since he thought I was going to sleep.

Naira seemed delighted, for I could see a slight smirk on her face.

No sooner did the three of us sit down, that Karan lit his cigarette. "Phuuu! he let out a cloud of smoke...this feels nice and warm"," Karan said cheerfully.

"Eee... it feels awful, I don't like the smell of cigarettes and it makes me feel sick. Karan, please can you go to the other side to smoke?" Naira requested him, though in an annoyed tone.

"ok...ok...I am going away...don't worry Naira," with this Karan signalled to me and moved away from us.

The two of us were left alone with a deadly silence. None of us spoke a word. After about five minutes, I initiated a conversation. "Look at the sky, Naira, illuminated by millions of stars. So far away, yet they seem to be so near. Isn't it a lovely sight?" I looked at her.

There was a twinkle in her eyes. "Yes, it's a beautiful view," she replied, to my surprise.

She went on, "I like the darkness of the night, for one can see the stars only in the darkness. I think it gives all of us a message - that there is light despite all the darkness in life. We should not lose hope under any circumstances, because the stars will come out and shine!"

I was impressed by what she said. How true it was, but surprisingly we still feared the darkness, we feared our failures and lost hope during our worst times. And I was the perfect example at that moment, living my life of hell... holding on to those grudges...those memories...that face. Not thinking that there may be a ray of hope somewhere for me...in the form of someone. But I couldn't see anything in the present circumstances. I had fallen into a deep dark hole somewhere all alone. Deep down, I was still grieving in that hole. I couldn't rise. I couldn't come up. I felt a tear trickling down my eyes. I moved away from Naira to hide my emotions. I couldn't understand how this girl was able to read my mind. I moved further away and wiped away the tears which had formed in my eyes.

Meanwhile, I heard Karan coming back after his smoke. He came and sat close to Naira and was whispering something in her ears. I gazed at them for some time. They were looking good together. Somehow, Naira spotted the empty rum bottle I had stashed away. She asked if it was mine and I simply nodded.

"Let's play a game,"' Naira said in a commanding voice looking at me and Karan. "Anyways, we are not feeling sleepy," she continued. Karan and I looked at each other, astonished at her tone.

"What game?" Karan was the first to ask.

"A game, now? At this hour of the night?" I retorted.

"Are you nuts, Naira?" both of us asked in unison.

"Yes and no. Guys we are not able to sleep. Then let's just play a game. A simple game of truth and dare, but today we will only play for truth," saying this she indicated the empty rum bottle in her hand.

"I hope you guys know the rules," she questioned.

"Of course," Karan was quick to reply.

Naira looked at me questioningly. I nodded my head. I knew this game but didn't want to play it now. I started fidgeting with my mobile.

"You don't have an option, Rihen. You have to play with us. Karan, only you can convince him," Naira insisted.

I still didn't budge.

She suddenly came close to me, snatched my mobile from my hands and took a few steps back.

"Naira, give my mobile back to me," I exclaimed angrily.

"First you promise to play the game," she glared at me.

"Please, Naira, it's a request. Give me my phone," I pleaded with her.

"Even I am requesting you," she was adamant.

Karan was watching all the drama between us. He didn't wish to become a prey to Naira's temper and thought it best not to interfere.

I realised that Naira was very keen for me to join in their game. Somehow even I wanted to play and pass my time. So, sensing that I had no other option, I finally gave in. "Okay, I'll play," saying this I sat down near the campfire which was now almost on the verge of burning out.

"Promise?" Naira held out her hand to me.

"Yeah promise," I replied grudgingly while giving my hand.

Karan and Naira sat opposite me. Karan looked very excited to play the game. He was stealing glances at Naira. She was staring at me. And I was looking at the empty rum bottle. Finally, Karan picked it up and spun the empty bottle. My heart skipped a beat while the bottle was spinning. 'Not me, not me...' I was thinking to myself, praying hard that my turn doesn't come.

The bottle stopped spinning. Through my half-closed eyes I peered to find that the bottle was pointing at Naira and the other end was towards Karan. 'Aah...thank God.' I was very happy it wasn't me. My heart resumed its normal beating.

"So, I have to ask Naira a question, right?" Karan was beaming with excitement. Naira looked amused. As usual, I was just a silent observer.

Karan looked at Naira and asked her, "So, what do you do Ms Naira? And, do you have a boyfriend?"

"Ohh...that's really smart, asking me two questions sat the same time, huh," Naira replied with a smile.

"Is it? So, you agree that I am smart?" Karan flirted with her.

"Of course," she replied.

"Okay, so, I am Naira from Ahmedabad. I finished my Fashion Designing course and am now working with a Fashion Designer in Ahmedabad. And no, I don't have a boyfriend. Does my answer satisfy you?" She asked Karan, but was looking at me. Karan gave her a broad smile.

"Wow! Fashion Designer ...sounds great." Karan answered, looking impressed.

"Thanks, but I have just started my career...let's see where it takes me," she replied.

With this, Karan rotated the bottle again and this time also it stopped between Naira and him. Only this time the bottle pointed towards Karan and the other end was towards Naira. Now, it was her turn to ask him a question. I heaved a sigh of relief for being saved a second time.

"So Naira, shoot a question," Karan prompted her.
"Wait, let me think...hmmm," Naira replied thoughtfully.
"Do you like someone?" Naira asked curiously.

"To be honest, I have liked many girls in the past. In school, I found the girl sitting next to me very cute and liked her a lot. In college, I had a crush on one of my juniors. Now I am a full-time photographer, so I get to meet many models during their photo shoot. I am working in a photography studio in Vadodara. As a matter of fact, I like many of my models. So, there is no one particular girl I can mention. I hope this satisfies you?" Karan gave a detailed reply.

"I meant liking someone seriously, like falling in love," Naira corrected him.
"Haha...now you are acting smart Naira...only one question per round...this I will answer next time," Karan teased her.
"Why don't you ask him, Rihen?' Naira nudged me.

I had a blank look. I wasn't interested in Karan's love life. Why would I want to know more about it? "Well, Karan is right. Only one question per round and I think he has answered." I don't know why I supported Karan. But I felt he answered his part very honestly.

"Okay, well whatever," Naira agreed reluctantly.

This time Naira rotated the bottle. I became nervous again, I prayed to God to save me a third time but unfortunately this time God didn't listen to my prayers. When I peeked through my half open eyes, the bottle was pointing towards me and the other half at Naira. I got scared knowing that Naira could ask me anything. Although I knew what she would ask?

"What is the reason behind your change of behaviour, Rihen?" Naira probed.

Yes, so I was right in judging her. I knew this was coming. I guessed right. For five minutes I didn't answer.

"Hey Rihen, please say something. Are you playing?" Naira tugged at my shoulder.

"No, I don't want to play," I answered.

"But you had promised me that you will play." It seemed as if Naira was almost on the verge of tears. I hate this side of girls, blackmailing people with their tears.

Sensing that Naira was upset, Karan held her in his arms. Taking her side, he said, "Common yaar Rihen, be a sport and answer her question."

"But I don't want to," I retorted.

"It's just a short and simple question. Why don't you just answer it and get on with the game?" Like me, Karan seemed disinterested in my life. What would he do knowing the truth behind my story?

But Naira was adamant. She would not move ahead without first getting an answer to her question. After a lot of coaxing and pleading from both of them, I finally surrendered. I had no option but to speak as I had promised Naira. I had to tell her the reason behind the sudden change in my behaviour. Go back to all the events I had been trying to escape from. Dig into the past I was hiding from everyone. Slowly, I gathered courage, closed my eyes and started speaking, unfolding the events of my past before Naira and Karan.

7

Past

It was the month of romance, I mean the month of February. It had been a few days since I had come back from my first ever trekking trip. It had been an incredible experience in the Dang Forest. I had gone with my friends and we had enjoyed every moment of it. I came back rejuvenated. It was a precious memory which will last for a lifetime. Once back, I had got into my normal routine and going to work at my father's factory, hanging out with friends, going to movies with my sister Nisha and the usual everyday life.

One day after dinner, I was sitting with my laptop, browsing through my social media pages. I had uploaded many photos from my trekking trip. Subsequent to the trek, there were innumerable friend requests from people I had met on the trip. Some of them I recalled, few I couldn't remember meeting. Some requests were from friends of friends. I got many likes also on my pictures. In short, I got an overwhelming response for my trekking trip and people from different corners became friends with me in the virtual world. While browsing through my Homepage, I found a friend suggestion. The name on the page read Aaruhi. I had never heard of her before. But her DP looked very attractive. I was tempted to see her profile. I checked her profile. It was full of pictures of this gorgeous beauty. Her deep-set black eyes, the rosy lips, her fair chubby face and long silky tresses immediately caught my attention. I remained glued on the screen for another five minutes. I looked at her photos again and again, continuously scrolling up and down through her profile. Yes, Aaruhi's beauty left me awe-struck. It was as if the face was saying something to me, something interesting. Her demeanour was breath-taking and it seemed to be beckoning me. It was as if deep in those ebony eyes, a dream undoubtedly a fascinating one – was waiting to be unfolded. I was curious to know more about this pretty girl who had completely smitten me in the first look. I just could not take my eyes off her. Just then my sister barged into my room to take a book and I sprang up in surprise. I immediately closed my laptop because I knew my little sister had this habit of peeping. I didn't want her to get any weird ideas if she saw that I was looking at a girl's picture like this.

"What were you doing?" she asked casually.

"Nothing, just scrolling through Facebook." I replied in a normal tone.

"So why did you just shut it off?" she asked bluntly.

"What...?"

"Oh, you mean the laptop? Well, I got bored so I closed it." I wanted to go back to Aaruhi and waited anxiously for my sister to go out of my room.

"What do you want?" I asked her.

"Your encyclopaedia," she replied.

"It's right there on the shelf," I told her impatiently.

"Yeah, I got it. Thanks brother. See you in a while," she said flippantly.

"See you in the morning," I replied. "And close the door of my room" I added.

She chuckled but closed the room behind her.

Pheww...what a relief.

After she left, I immediately opened my laptop. Aaruhi was staring at me out of the screen. I went to her friends list which was huge. I found one or two mutual friends. Both of them were from my school. We had common school friends? Funny. I couldn't somehow recall that she was in my school. Now my curiosity got the better of me. I wanted to learn more about this mysterious girl on Facebook. More importantly, since she had sent me a friend request, I was all the more curious about her. I had this burning desire to befriend Aaruhi and talk to her. I accepted her friend request. Next, I randomly liked many of her pictures displayed on her profile. I also posted comments of 'looking nice' on some of the pictures I liked. She looked captivating in every photo. Her stunning beady eyes framed by dense long lashes made her face look beautiful beyond description, bewitching me every moment. I was friends with many girls, but never had I felt attracted to anyone like this before. This was the first time that I felt an instant attraction for a girl. But then there was something mystical about Aaruhi. Her big black eyes had hooked me. I couldn't sleep properly that night. I kept thinking about this mysterious girl and wanted to know her better. I wanted to talk to her, to feel her, to touch her...to ....and then slowly I drifted into a deep sleep. Dreaming about us... me and Aaruhi together.

Every day I would check my Facebook page to see if Aaruhi had responded to my comments. I wanted to find out if she had noticed that I had accepted her friend request. I would scroll through her profile every alternate day just to see her pretty face. Seeing her, even though only on the laptop screen, would brighten me. I couldn't help but notice her silky lustrous strands dangling over her slightly lighter than ivory round face. It looked as if she was also staring back at only me. As if she was made just for me. So perfect, yet so frustrating that I could have no contact with this sensuous girl. It had been two days but she hadn't shown any response. Damn it. I wanted to talk to her, know her, feel her...and my fondness for her was getting more intense day by day. Meanwhile, I also befriended our mutual friend – the one from my school. I came to know from this common friend that she had joined our school in the 11th class. I had left school in the 10th class to join a diploma course. So, she had joined school after I left. Since she was from my school and we had common friends, I was sure I could easily relate to her and talk to her.

Three days later, I was casually checking my Facebook once again, when I saw that she had liked my likes. And there was more. She had even sent a 'Hi' on messenger. I was on cloud nine. I was so happy that I started jumping on my bed. My sister who was sleeping in the next room came in to check on me. "What happened bro?" she asked.

"Nothing," I replied. But I couldn't contain my excitement. It was quite visible from my body language.

When she had come to my room, my arms were swaying in the air, I was dancing haphazardly, my hair was tousled and I had a bemused look on my face.

"It's nothing, okay. I was just having a funny conversation with one of my friends. That's it. Now you go back to sleep," and I nudged her out of my room.

I shut the door of my room and switched off the lights and lay down on my massive fluffy bed. Once on the bed, I immediately installed the Facebook messenger App on my phone. It was 11 pm at night. Even today, I clearly remember the time for I was brimming with such excitement that day. She had sent a 'Hi' at 10.08 pm and now seemed to be offline. Nevertheless, I sent her a 'Hi' on messenger. I couldn't contain my excitement.

Five minutes later, I saw she was online. Aaruhi waved at me. I was surprised to get her reply so fast. My heart started beating nervously. I got anxious. The girl for whom I had been pinning for so many days had finally accepted my request and was even responding to me. I had moved one step ahead.

(Messenger chat)

Me – Hey, how are you?

Aaruhi - I am fine, what about you?

Me – Am fine.

Aaruhi - Why suddenly so many likes on my pictures?

Me – Your photos are amazing so I liked them.

Aaruhi – Oh only pictures right?

Me – Yeah of course. You know I was in your school?

Aaruhi – Oh, sorry I don't remember.

Me – Hmm, how will you remember me, I was not in your class.

Aaruhi – Oh then which class?

Me – No I mean I left after my 10th and you joined school then.

Aaruhi – Then how do you know that I was in your school?

Me –I know you through a common friend.

Aaruhi – Who?

Me – Hmmm. Yeah

Aaruhi – Oh okay. That's nice. So what are you doing nowadays? I mean study or job?

Me – Finished study, just joined dad's business. I work at my dad's factory. What about you?

Aaruhi - Study finished, now just chilling at home.

Me – oh! okay. Can you please tell me more about yourself?

Aaruhi –What do you want to know? Have you ever seen me?

Me – No but yeah, your display picture. I saw your profile on Facebook and liked it.

Aaruhi – Hmm ok.

Me- So what time do you sleep?

Aaruhi – Usually 11 pm but nothing fixed, you?

Me – Same, actually not fixed, it is on my mood. If any interesting conversation is going on then, I don't see the time. Can I give you an example?

Aaruhi – Yeah

Me - Like now, you know its 12am.

Aaruhi – Oh yeah, I didn't notice. I better go to sleep then.

Me - Hey wait, what's the hurry. We still haven't talked properly.

Aaruhi – We will again, someday soon. Okay bye.

Me – Okay good night. Catch you tomorrow.

(Chat ends)

At first I was a bit upset that she came online only for five minutes. Obviously, I couldn't sleep the whole night. I was brimming with happiness. I had goose bumps all over my body. I didn't know what to do or how to react. I was feeling so very happy. Finally, I had had a chat with the girl I so longed to talk to. She seemed quite amazing too. I kept tossing in my bed, thinking of her, dreaming of her... wanting to be with her. Uff...I knew I was overreacting for it was just a casual chat. But I couldn't get Aaruhi out of my head. After so many days of wanting to talk to her I had finally got my chance. I also knew we would chat again soon.

My forecast came true within two days.

(Messenger chat)

Aaruhi – Good morning!

Me – Hey good morning, how's you?

Aaruhi – Am good, you tell?

me – Am also fine.

Aaruhi – So where do you live?

Me – At my house.

Aaruhi – Haha, it's a terrible joke.

Me – I stay in Surat. What about you?

Aaruhi – Right now am living in a village near Navsari.

Me – Oh okay

Aaruhi – So with whom do you live, I mean how many people are there in your family?

Me – We are four - my parents, my younger sister and myself.

Aaruhi – Nice. I'm living with my Nana-Nani and younger brother.

Me – Ohh and what about your mom & dad?

Aaruhi – It's a long story, will tell you later.

Me – Okay and what is your younger brother doing?

Aaruhi – He is studying in 11th class.

Me – Oh okay.

Aaruhi – Now I have to prepare lunch. bye see you soon. What's your lunch time?

Me – At 1 & your lunch time seems too early.

Aaruhi – Ya, it's a village so all things are done early.

Me – You don't look like you live in a village.

Aaruhi – Then how do I look?

Me – (silent no answer)

Aaruhi – Actually I came here five years ago due to certain circumstances, otherwise I was in Surat only.

Me – Oh, ok. So what happened?
Aaruhi – That story also we will keep for later. Okay I'm going bye.
Me – Okay take care.

Next day we again chatted for some time in the morning. This went on for a few days.

(On the fifth day of our chat)
Aaruhi - Hi Rihen, whats up?
Me - Hi Aaruhi. Just going to work. What are you doing?

(Since then, there was no reply. I waited desperately for her message. But there was no answer. I checked and rechecked my phone several times. Then I got ready to go for work as I was getting late. But I was very anxious and I became more anxious with every passing minute. There were many questions in my mind. If she had seen my message, why had she not responded? What must have happened? I thought of messaging her again but didn't do so. I waited and waited. Finally, my patience bore results in the evening.)

Incoming Video call (from Aaruhi) 7:27 pm

I couldn't believe my eyes. Video call from her! Oh my God! I looked at myself in the mirror to check my appearance. My shirt was out of my pants and my face looked weary. The call had ended by then. It doesn't matter, I thought to myself. I will call her back. I quickly washed my face, straightened my hair, tucked my shirt in and settled down in a corner with a good background. The phone started to ring again. I was very nervous. I double checked to make sure I was looking good. The phone was still ringing. Then I answered the video call.

Me – Hey!
(Wow! It was the first time that I saw her. She looked prettier on screen, prettier than her pictures. Her big bold round pearly eyes mesmerised me).

Aaruhi – Sorry I didn't reply, I was busy at that time. Also, I was at my friend's house and had forgotten my charger at home and my phone went dead. So, I couldn't reply the entire day. Later I went out with my friend for shopping and just came back home half an hour ago and thought of calling you.
(She was speaking non-stop like a superfast express train. She was telling me everything so quickly that I couldn't grasp half the things, but I liked the way she was talking).

Me – Oh, okay, slow down and relax. Not a problem. I was thinking about why you didn't reply and what had happened. But now that you have told me, I am relaxed. Just chill.
Aaruhi – Yeah, but I was feeling guilty as I had not replied to your message.
Me – It's okay. I understand.

There was a pause for a moment.

Then I told her "By the way, you are much more pretty than your pictures."
Aaruhi – Oh really! thank you! Many people have told me the same thing. In fact, many guys follow me.
There was a hint of pride in her voice.
Me - Hmm...good...and did you like any of them?

Aaruhi - Why?

Me – Generally, asking.

Aaruhi - Lol...what do you think?

Me - I don't know. That is why I am asking you.

Aaruhi– Hey, are the Barbers on strike there?

Me – No, why?

I was surprised at how swiftly she changed the topic.

Aaruhi – Then why have you kept your beard and hair so long?

Me - Haha, I like it that way. You don't like it?

Aaruhi - Does it matter? We are hardly friends we are more of strangers.

Me - Yet we are talking like friends, isn't it?

Aaruhi –True.

Me - Sometimes strangers become the best of friends and your best friends may become like strangers.

Aaruhi - Woahhh...that's too deep. I like what you just said.

Me - Anyway, soon I will shave my beard. anything else?

Aaruhi – Nothing. I have to go, Nani is calling.

Me –Wait.

Aaruhi– Bye.

Me – Okay,tc bye.

Video call ended *7:58 pm*

A few days later, we were again chatting on the phone. It seemed that we already couldn't do without each other. Initially, we were just strangers, but once we started talking to each other, we just couldn't stop. It was as if some unknown force was binding us together.

Messenger Chats (11.30 pm)

Me: *Hi, it was nice to see you in the evening.*
Aaruhi - *Same here.*
Me - *Had dinner?*
Aaruhi - *Yeah, long back. Remember, here we have early lunch and early dinner.*
Me - *Hmm...so what are you doing?*
Aaruhi - *Nothing was watching TV, now relaxing in my room. You tell?*
Me - *I was playing with my sister a while ago and now in my room too. Can I tell you something?*
Aaruhi - *Yes please, tell me.*
Me - *I like your eyes a lot.*
Aaruhi - *Oh really?*
Me - *Yeah.*
Aaruhi - *Oh thanks. (She posted a smiley emoticon for the first time).*
Me - *(I also put a smiley emoticon).*
Aaruhi - *So what do you like about my eyes?*
Me - *I love how deep your black eyes look...so innocent.*
Aaruhi - *Oh thank you :) but you are the first one to say this...*
Me- *What? That I like your eyes?*
Aaruhi - *No, that they are innocent. I like it. (She gave a loud laugh).*

Back then, I didn't understand why she laughed like that.

Aaruhi- *Did you like anyone else before?*
Me - *No. (And that was the truth)*
But I have many female friends.
Aaruhi - *Then why have you put up so many depressive questions on your profile page.*

(The questions were:
1. What is more important - love or friendship?
2. Why being honest in a relationship breaks it??)

Me - Oh that is nothing. Ignore that.
Aaruhi - No, please tell me.
Me- Really you wouldn't be interested in knowing. It's about my school gang of friends.
Aaruhi - I want to know about it. Please tell me.
Me - It is late at night.
Aaruhi - I know it's almost 12am and I sleep every day max by 10:30 pm, but today I didn't realise the time while I was talking with you. Wait I will do a video call.

I felt elated upon hearing this.

Incoming Video call *(from Aaruhi) 12:05am*

Me- We were a group of three close friends. Guys only. We were together since school. We never hide anything from each other. Life was going smoothly till the other 2 made girlfriends. At first, we were happy to add them in our group and we liked them. Slowly our group dynamics changed. The two couples went out together, not inviting me. Love changed the equation between our friendship. Initially, I thought this was normal. But day by day I felt left out. They started hiding things from me. Whenever we met, I was made the scapegoat since I was the only single guy. They made a laughing stock out of my single status.

Even the girls would make fun of me. They even tried to set me up with their friends, but I never liked anyone. One day I did not like something that my friend's girlfriend said. I immediately rebuked her for it. She felt bad and got very upset. She went away from there. My friend went after her to pacify her. The other two also blamed me for my rude behaviour. But I knew in my heart that she was wrong and what I said was right. Anyway, I left it at that. It was not my fault, but everything ended in misunderstandings between us. From that day, I gradually distanced myself from my friends.

Me - During that time when I was undergoing this emotional turmoil with my friends, I wrote those questions on my profile to vent out my frustration. It's been some time now. We three are on talking terms but we are not as close as we were before. That's about it. And yeah, nobody can answer those questions.

Aaruhi – I have answers to all your questions
Me – Then tell me one by one.
Aaruhi – Not today. It is very late now. But will definitely answer your questions.
Me – Okay.
Aaruhi – Goodnight, Rihen!
Me – Good night. Take care, sweet dreams.
Aaruhi – See you next time. Take care, good night.
Me – Tomorrow?

But she had already ended the video call.

I felt very light after talking to Aaruhi about my friends that day. As if some burden had been lifted out from my heart. Smiling to myself, I immediately went off to sleep.

(Back to the present at the camp)

"Hello Naira." I said, waving both my hands in front of her face. She was in a statue mode. "Hello, Hello!" I shook my hands again in front of her almost hypnotised eyes. Her eyes were glaring at me and I felt as if my bones were freezing, like being naked in the middle of a hailstorm. Then she blinked and the beauty of her eyes was momentarily covered by the shield of her naturally long and soft looking eyelashes.

"It's 1am, we have to wake up early tomorrow," I told her.

"Yeah, but it was interesting and I want to know further," Naira finally broke her silence.

Karan was looking blank. He had no reaction whatsoever.

"Naira, I will tell you my story. But not right now. It is getting late. And we have a long trek tomorrow. Please understand, I'm feeling sleepy. I'm going. Good night," I said.

Karan, sitting next to Naira, agreed with me. I looked at Karan who was continuously watching Naira. Soon we bade goodnight to each other and departed to our tents.

8

Jealousness

Next morning the usual gong rang for us to wake up. I was feeling sleepy and just couldn't open my eyes. Being awake till late night had taken its toll on me. Since we were four of us in the tent, I could hear the sounds of other boys waking up and talking amongst themselves. Lakshya came and removed my blanket to wake me up. "Get up buddy, today it's a long trek. Get up or you will be late. And then you know...blah blah..."

Lakshya had so much to blabber in the morning too...I didn't listen to any more of his jabbering and instead pulled my blanket over my face and went off to sleep again. Fifteen minutes later, I heard some peculiar loud noises and woke up. My eyes were still puffy due to the sleeplessness of the night before. I looked around the tent. There was no one. Maybe it was some animal around the tent. I was just about to pull my blanket over my head again and nod off when I sleepily looked at my mobile to see the time. It was almost 6.30 am. 'Gosh, I need to be quick, or else I will be late.' I muttered half asleep. I was wondering if Naira and Karan were also as sleepy as me or had they already woken up. I heard that peculiar sound again and this time it seemed to be coming from the tent. I searched for the source of that unusual sound in the tent, outside the tent but could find nothing. I thought I must be dreaming. 'Now, hurry up Rihen', I reminded myself. I quickly brushed my teeth and freshened up with just two mugs of cold water. Putting on a tight sweatshirt, baggy pants and my favourite jacket I went outside.

It was bright and sunny. The rays of the sun immediately lifted my mood and made me cheerful. Most of the trekkers had gathered around the breakfast table. "Good morning, buddy," Karan wished me as soon as I went towards the gang. I was taken aback by his friendly tone. He looked a bit disinterested yesterday and we had hardly talked to each other. But today, it was as if he had become my bestie. I looked up at him. He appeared as fresh as dew and as fit as a horse. How could he be so fresh after sleeping so late at night? I wanted to ask him but did not do so at that point.

I just replied back with a 'Good Morning'. He came closer to me and whispered in my ears, "You know what, Naira is still sleeping. That beautiful lass is going to be punished today."

"Oh no, she has still not woken up?" I felt concerned. "If she is late, she will definitely be punished. We should do something," I told Karan.

"I agree. That is why I am going to her tent to wake up that sleeping beauty," saying this he winked at me.

"But shouldn't we tell one of the girls to wake her up? I don't suppose boys are allowed to go into the girls tent..." But before I could even finish what I was saying, Karan just shrugged and went away towards Naira's tent. He had just called her sleeping beauty. So, he found Naira beautiful too. Well, she was that was for sure. Any guy would fall for her dimpled smile. But I don't know why this little thought disturbed me. Had Karan developed a liking for Naira?

All my cheerfulness vanished into thin air. My mood suddenly changed from happy to sad. Was I getting jealous? Or was I reacting too much? Had I also fallen for Naira? No...no... It's not possible. I brushed away my wild thoughts.

I looked towards Naira's tent. Karan was still inside and they both had not come out. Well, maybe they weren't wild thoughts. I was indeed disturbed, jealous, worried all at the same time. My thoughts were interrupted by a shout from Raju Sir. He signalled me to come and join him. I immediately went over to him. He was having his tea with Ching Sir. I took my cup of hot ginger tea and joined them.

"Hello, Good Morning Sirs", I greeted them both.

"Good morning Rihen, you are late today," it was more a statement than a question.

"Yes Sir, sorry I overslept," I replied sheepishly.

"No problem. Now listen, get ready quickly. Today, our trek will be rough. Plus, there is also a possibility of rain," Raju Sir told me.

"But it doesn't look like it's going to rain anytime soon," I pointed towards the bright golden sun casting its warm rays across the clear blue sky.

"The weather can be very uncertain here. I have a feeling that it's going to rain today," Ching Sir cautioned me.

"Hmmm... okay," I didn't know what else to say.

"Since you have been on a trek earlier, I want you to support us in case there is any need during the trek. I want you to help with the distribution of ponchos to protect ourselves from the rainy weather."

"Sure Sir, anytime you need me, I will be there," I replied with a smile.

Later, we had hot steamy parathas, potato sabzi, chutney and pickle for breakfast. All of us were discussing the today's trek. Most of us knew it was going to be a tough trek. We made sure to store our energy by filling up our stomachs with the yummy parathas. I spotted Naira coming out of her tent for breakfast. She looked so pretty in the morning sun. Her cheeks had become as red as the colour of apples. But her face looked weary and her hair was all messed up. Behind her, Karan came out. They both were coming towards where I was standing.

I went close to her and whispered softly in her ears, "No more late nights now".

She was surprised by my closeness. With a smirk on her face, she looked at me funnily and said, "I want to know more some way or the other. I will see how it works out". Saying this she went towards the breakfast table. I overhead Ching Sir scolding her for being late regularly. As usual,

Karan was there to support her. I moved away from there and went to my tent.

Back in the tent, I saw that everyone was hurriedly packing their things. Since we were moving to the next camp, we had to pack our stuff. For the next few minutes we all got into a playful mood, throwing our smelly socks and unwashed clothes on each other. Later we all ended up falling onto each other. The guy at the bottom was shrieking to let go of his hand...but we continued with our friendly romping. All this naughtiness helped to uplift my mood. It helped me overcome the pain I had been enduring for the past few months. With friends in the trek (Naira too) I was slowly coming back to my normal self. Since the events that had occurred in my life, I had stopped trusting anyone outside my immediate family. I didn't feel like talking to anyone. I had enclosed myself into a shell. But after meeting Naira, I had slowly started opening that shell, though I still didn't fully trust her. But I somehow knew she had a heart of gold and that she wouldn't hurt even a fly. Her beautiful and innocent face attracted me. But I was cautious. I didn't want to make a fool of myself again. 'I will not express any emotions this time', I had decided. I didn't want to be hurt a second time.

At 8.00 am sharp we all gathered our belongings and set-off towards our next destination. The energy among the group was high. We trailed through long winding roads, sometimes with steep bends or small waterfalls through the cuts in the rocky hills. Chattering, listening to the sound of birds, singing, we all climbed up the mountains in a single line, sticking to our routine.

After walking for some time, we finally stopped near a rocky enclave. We knew this was a stopover point for some kind of activity. Ching Sir took out his big fleece jacket and put it on the nearby rock. Flexing his hands, he warmed himself and then addressed the group, "So team, behind me you can see a long wire like rope with two end points. We are going to do the zip-line activity today. There is a narrow swinging bridge just besides it. After finishing the zip-line, you have to come back to this side by walking on the narrow foot bridge". There was murmuring in the group. I had done it before and so had Karan and some other guys. Lakshya had never attempted this before and looked horrified.

"It's easy," I managed to calm him.

Many of the girls were quite excited to do the zip-lining adventure. But most of the members were apprehensive as they were attempting it for the first time. The long single wire, the deep abyss, the tall treetops surrounding the cliffs...everything looked thrilling but scary.

Sensing our fear and excitement, Ching Sir further continued, "Team, I assure you this will be one of your most exciting adventures. Zip-lining is a fun, fast and thrilling activity! All you need to do is strap on a harness, clip onto the line and you are ready to go. You can catch some amazing views and feel an adrenaline rush as you zip through the tree tops and along the edge of the cliffs. There is nothing to worry about. Everyone will be fastened safely to the zip-line. Our professionals here have already inspected the cables, anchor points and other equipment that will be used during the course of this activity. They will now guide you on how to exactly travel on the zip-line and enjoy the adventure. Meanwhile, I will also give you a quick short demonstration and you all can follow me one by one".

'So, are you all ready for this new thrilling adventure?" Ching and Raju Sirs asked together.

"Yes," we all replied loudly.

"Good, then I will be going first. See you all on the opposite side of the camp." Saying this, we watched in utter amazement as Ching Sir put on the safety equipment, strapped himself to the line and zoomed away on the zip-line. It looked as if he was flying like a free bird in the huge open sky. He waved and cheered loudly from the opposite side.

We were given a short demonstration by some local professionals. Then Raju Sir asked us to form a line, boys and girls together and ordered us to proceed on the zip-line one by one.

Lakshya, Karan, Naira, her two friends and me assembled together and stood next to each other.
    "I am very nervous," Lakshya said fearfully.
    "We too," Naira's two friends added.
    "Guys, it's going to be fun. Trust me. You will enjoy the zip-line alot. Just don't look down, look around at the beautiful surroundings and views." Naira said this to all three of them.

Karan agreed. I nodded my head. We could hear the same fear amongst the other group members as well.

"What if my cable breaks off in the middle? What if my harness comes off? What if I fall down?" Everyone had so many questions whirling in their minds. Raju Sir along with another professional member patiently answered all the queries.

"Last time we did zip-lining over a river. It was fun, wasn't it, Rihen?" Naira was beaming at me.

"Yeah, I felt like a bird flying over a gulping river stream below. Being a first experience made it all the more exciting. I can imagine how you all are feeling right now." I replied to her while addressing the others.

"Wow, you guys are lucky. I have done zip-lining twice but not over a river." Karan chipped in.

Later, Naira went on with her friends.

Everyone was discussing the correct posture for the zip-line adventure - what to do, what not to do, how to hold, how to swing and other endless ways to cross the cable.

Just as I was heading towards Naira, I heard Raju Sir calling my name. I went off in his direction.

"Rihen, I would request you and Naira to go first as you have previously done this. Looking at you, I am sure the others will be assured about its safety. Please go and call Naira,' Raju Sir told me.

"Yes Sir," I was already feeling excited and now my excitement level shot up on hearing this.

"Naira...Naira..." I shouted her name and when she looked in my direction, I signalled for her to come and join me. She quickly came towards me. Together we went to Raju Sir, who gave her the same instructions as he had given me.

We went ahead of the line and I volunteered to go first. I put on the harness, strapped, fastened and clipped my jacket and steadied my posture. Ready, get set and go...and off I zoomed away. That same exhilarating feeling, flying high in the sky like a bird over the cliffs and the great expanse of dense forest. Wow! What an amazing feeling it was. I leaned back and spread my legs in the air while swinging hundreds of metres high up in the air. My heart was beating fast but a huge smile appeared on my face as I was thrust forward through the air in the direction of the magnificent Himalayan peaks. Faster and faster I went. And then before I knew it, the zip-line came to an end. I reached the other end. How I wished that the zip-line had been a little longer so I could treat my eyes to the majestic mountain peaks. But I knew this would last only a few minutes.

I then, waited patiently for Naira to join me. I could see her strapping her jacket, getting into position and here she comes ...wide-eyed and hair flying in the air, she was screaming in excitement. But suddenly her zip-line slowed down a bit half-way through the air. Naira's happy screams suddenly turned into panic. I got nervous too. For a moment, it seemed that Naira had got stuck in mid-air. The wind was swaying her slightly to the left and then slightly to the right. From the opposite end, Raju Sir signalled to Ching Sir to stay calm. Naira took us all by surprise. She used all her strength to keep the harness in position, leaned back, pulled both the ropes to release and pushed herself forward. And slowly she started moving forward, few metres ahead she regained her motion and came zipping down fast towards us. As soon as she landed, I went towards her and she gave me an embarrassing look.

"I could have done better. Really...I was looking like such a fool swinging in the middle of the rope. And this was my second time. I could have done better...oh no..." Naira continued blabbering to me.

"Relax," I told her calmly.

"And you have to continue telling me your story," Naira reminded me softly.

Just then we saw the next team member coming through the zip-line. One by one all of them landed on the other side. Everyone except Lakshya had fun doing the zip-line adventure. Lakshya, like Naira, had got stuck in the middle for a few moments and had panicked. He wasn't too happy with his experience.

Next, we all had to go back to our starting point by walking on the narrow bridge just next to our zip-line. It was a wooden bridge with planks just wide enough for one foot. There were ropes on both sides to hold on to. All of us thought it would be easy and fun and we would finish in a few minutes, just like the zip-line. After all we only had to walk. Until we saw Ching Sir walking slowly on the bridge, one foot after the other and to our horror, the light wooden bridge was swinging furiously from left to right.

"Oh my God!" Lakshya gasped in horror. Others were equally horrified. But Raju Sir assured us that it wouldn't be as difficult as it looked. This time Karan volunteered to go first and Raju Sir readily agreed. The girls cheered Karan and wished him luck. Karan looked pleased with the attention he was getting. He assured all of them that since he had done this before, he would be fine. In fact, he even started giving foot demonstrations to the girls on how they should walk on the bridge. Indeed, when he stepped on the bridge, he started walking effortlessly. The bridge was swinging very hard and it looked very dangerous. But Karan managed to reach the other end very smoothly and showed a thumbs-up sign to all of us from there. He had a big grin on his face. He was followed by some girls, next were some boys, then Naira, myself and finally Lakshya was the last to come. Most of us were able to cross the foot bridge with ease following the instructions given by Raju Sir. Some of us got stuck, some girls screamed now and then, but eventually we all made it to the other end. Fortunately, even Lakshya was able to cross the bridge easily and was quite pleased with himself. He was happily sharing his experience with me and some other guys on how he overcame his fear and enjoyed this adventure.

Once everyone reached, we settled down near the site. Lunch was served to us. We all devoured the parathas, pakoda curry, sabzi and salad and ate to our satisfaction. After lunch, we were given five minutes to assemble our rucksacks and get ready for the onward hike. It was almost 3 pm when we started our trek again. We hiked high through the mountains, across the plains and slowly neared our next campsite.

Mid-way through the trek, during early afternoon the weather suddenly changed. At first there was a light drizzle, but it was soon followed by a heavy downpour. Some of the members ran here and there for shelter, some of us rejoiced in the rain, a few were dancing with delight in the heavy downpour. Though we all took out our ponchos, it was a bit late as the heavy downpour soaked us through and through. All of us got fully wet, including our clothes and bags, and the uncalled rain left us all shivering!

Ching Sir blew a loud whistle and asked us to quickly follow him. Ten minutes later we all gathered near a cave rock. It was the best shelter that Sir could find within that short time. We had to wait there till the rains slowed down. I remembered that in the morning while having breakfast, I had expressed my doubts to Raju Sir and Ching Sir on whether it will rain or not. They had been proved right. The weather was very unpredictable here. Most of us were wet and shivering. Just then Ching Sir had an idea. He went over to Raju Sir and discussed something with him. Raju Sir nodded in agreement. It was dark and a little eerie inside the cave. They both went further inside the cave, searched for signs of any animals and when they were sure of its safety, they went to the centre of the cave and lit a huge bonfire. All of us followed both of them inside the cave.

"Team, we will spend some time here till the rain subsides," Ching Sir informed us.

Initially there was a loud murmur in the group as this stop would mean that our hike would be delayed by a few hours and we would reach late at our campsite. Nevertheless, after the thrilling zip-lining adventure, spending time in the cave turned out to be more exhilarating. It was just that most of us were freezing with cold and shivering from getting wet in the sudden downpour. The boys removed their T-shirts and changed on the spot. It was easy for guys to do so. Seeing that the boys had changed, the girls also had an idea. The girls formed a big circle and held out their shawls and jackets, while each one took turns to change into dry clothes. So, now we were all dry and comfortable.

To dry out our wet clothes, we spread the shirts and sweaters and some of our track pants on the stones in the cave. It looked funny, as if there was a sale for T-shirts and jackets. Though it was a colourful sight for a dark rainy day! We formed a large circle around the bonfire and started chit chatting. The fire warmed us. The cave was filled with campfire and booming laughter as Lakshya kept everyone enthralled with funny stories. Soon, everyone started sharing their own stories of adventure. It was fun listening to everyone's experience. We didn't realise when an hour had passed. With little hope of the rains slowing down, the cooking staff made light snacks for us. We were relieved to be treated to steamy masala Maggi noodles with hot and sour tomato soup. It was heartily welcomed in this rainy weather. We all ate to our heart's content.

Since it was still raining, Raju Sir suggested that we all rest there till the downpour stopped completely. He didn't want to risk or take any chances with the group. He along with Ching Sir went out to connect with our next campsite, which wasn't very far. Inside the cave, most of the members took a nap while some formed small groups and started playing dumb charades. I was about to take a nap and rest when I saw Karan and Naira coming towards me. Without a word of caution, Karan took my hand and together they dragged me to a far end corner of the cave where there was nobody. Both of them sat comfortably on the big boulders and instructed me to do the same. I was bewildered with their action and was just about to open my mouth to protest when Naira very sweetly and innocently said, "Please continue your story, Rihen. We are waiting to hear when you two met for the first time and what happened afterwards".

9

First Date

At first I was shocked and then realised that I had no choice. Naira's curiosity would never leave me without knowing the full story. But I didn't know Karan was also interested in my story. Or did he join in only because of Naira, so that he could spend more time with her, be close to her? I had my doubts where Karan was concerned. He wouldn't miss any opportunity to be with Naira. And this must be his golden opportunity. I glanced at the beautiful dimpled cute girl sitting with hopeful eyes in front of me. Then I glanced at Karan who showed no expression on his face apart from the fact that he was sitting quite close to Naira. I closed my eyes and remembered my first meeting with Aaruhi and continued my story.

We had been talking on the phone and video calls for almost a month. Not a day passed by when we would not talk. If one of us were busy in some work or the other, we would at least drop in a Hi or a goodnight message by the end of the day. It was as if we were already in love and were boyfriend-girlfriend.

After almost a month of chatting, I remember, it was Aaruhi who suggested one fine day that we should meet. Yes, I clearly remember that it was the night of 15th March. My sister's final board exams were going on. Nisha was studying till late at night. I would peek into her room just to see if she was awake, motivate her a bit and then come back to my room to chat with Aaruhi. Sometimes we would binge on snacks late at night, while she was studying. On that particular night, I was sitting in Nisha's room and having popcorn.

Just then a message flashed on my mobile screen. It read, 'let's meet Rihen".

At first I was amused, then I was happy and then my pulse started racing. My excitement knew no bounds. I started jumping up and down. I couldn't control my excitement. I was so happy. I was feeling on top of the world and started dancing in the room. Nisha looked at me in bewilderment and asked, "What's wrong brother?? Or should I ask what are you so happy about?" I had forgotten that I was with my sister in her room. I was taken aback by her presence and now her question.

"Nothing that concerns you little sis. It's just about one of my friends". I replied cheekily.
"Fine, if you do not wish to share with me. I always thought you were my friend more than a brother. But maybe I was wrong. You don't want to tell me, then don't. Even I'm not interested in hearing it. Go away," she said, evidently upset with me.

"Okay, I will tell you but not now, when the time is right. Anyway, you better concentrate on your exams. And yes, we are always friends first and then brother and sister. That will never change. You understand?" I gave her a pat on the cheek.

"Yes bro..." she replied with a sign of satisfaction and went back to her studies.

In all the excitement, I even forgot to reply to Aaruhi.

'Oh shit!' I muttered to myself.

"Okay bye Nisha, Goodnight. Best of luck for your exams," saying this I left her room and went to my room. The moment I came back to my room, I opened my mobile and replied to her.

(Messenger chat)

Me - Yes, I would like to meet you too :) (Followed by a smiley)

Aaruhi - What took you so long to reply huh???

Me - Nothing really, I was with my sister and just came to my room. Sorry, friend.

Aaruhi - It's okay, so when and where do we meet?

Me - Why don't you suggest?

Aaruhi - Let's meet at the cafe in Hilton Hotel.

Hilton Hotel was one of the best 4-star properties in our city. I also loved its café. Though it was expensive, I could very well afford it. But the only problem was that I frequented it with my family and friends and most of the staff there knew me well. I couldn't risk spoiling my first ever date with Aaruhi. No, I couldn't go there.

Me: Ahem...can we go somewhere else?

Aaruhi: Why? What is wrong with Hilton?

She was a bit abrupt.

Rihen: Nothing is wrong. In fact, I love the cafe.

Before I could type further, she replied.

Aaruhi: Then why are you saying no. Is it because it's too expensive?

Rihen: No, no...it's not that. The reason is...

Aaruhi: What's the reason?

Me: I'm trying to explain. Why don't you let me finish first? I sounded a bit irritated.

Aaruhi: Of course, go on. First you ask me to choose a place of meeting and then you say no.

Me: But I go there very often with my family and everyone knows me well. If I go with you, someone will recognise me and we can get into trouble. I don't want to spoil our first date.

Aaruhi: This seems like a lame excuse. Why don't you say you don't want to take me to the cafe? And even if someone recognises us, what's the big deal? Are you saying I embarrass you? That if you will be seen with me, you will feel embarrassed...huh?

Me: Hey...I never said anything like that. Please don't get me wrong.

Aaruhi: Now I'm taking it wrong :((Followed by a sad emoticon)

Me: No...no...I'm sorry if I hurt you. How can I be embarrassed by you? What you said is not true. In fact, I would like to introduce you to my family but not now. Let us enjoy our first date in a nice quiet place. Can I call you?

Aaruhi: No. I was so longing to go to Hilton Cafe.

Me: Okay, I promise to take you there, but some other time. This time let's go to some other place. Pleasssee...pleasssee.

Aaruhi: Okay, then you only suggest. What other option do I have?

Me: Let's meet at the Chai Cafe.

Aaruhi: What? That is such a tacky place. I didn't expect you to take me there for our first date.

Me: It's nice. I thought you might like it too.

Aaruhi: No, I don't go to such cheap places.

Me: Then you suggest something else.

(I was getting a bit frustrated. My excitement was dropping. I didn't know that deciding on the place for our first meeting would be so stressful.)

Aaruhi: Let us just drop the idea of a cafe. I don't want to go to a cafe now.

Me: Then where?

Aaruhi: Let's meet at the Lake Garden. It's a nice quiet spot.

Me: Okay. As you say.

I wasn't too keen. But I agreed as I didn't want to argue anymore.

Aaruhi: I hope you are saying it happily and not just to please me Rihen?

Me: Yes, yes, it's a nice place. I am quite excited.

Aaruhi: Cool then...3 pm tomorrow.

Me: Yes...I'm already super excited to see you :)

Aaruhi: Me too..bye...gn...

Me: See you tomorrow, gn... (I was about to type love you but deleted it.)

(Chat over)

I heaved a sigh of relief that finally our meeting place had been decided. Although I was quite surprised by how adamant she initially was for Hilton Cafe. Well, all is well now and tomorrow is going to be a super-duper day...I got lost in Aaruhi's thoughts...dreaming about our first meeting...dreaming about us...and slowly I drifted off into a deep, peaceful sleep.

Next day, I woke up early and shaved and styled my hair. I dressed, went to the factory but came back home early. The time went by very quickly. Before I knew it was lunch time, but I ate very little. Nisha again noticed my excitement but did not say anything. I was relieved. No sooner did we finish our lunch I went to my room to get ready.

Like every guy going on a first date, even I was standing in front of my open cupboard and was in a fix about what to wear. I scrutinized every inch of my cupboard which was full of branded clothes and accessories. Though I had picked up one or two casual clothes from the street, but I preferred only branded clothes. If one peeked into my closet, they will find two racks full of boots, sneakers, formal shoes and sandals. And yes, I am a lover of perfumes and had a collection of over 50 branded and exquisite perfumes from around the world.

What should I wear?? Oh God...I was so confused?

I stood for a good 10 minutes in front of my cupboard. I even tried on a few shirts and pants but rejected them all. Finally, my choice was between a white shirt and blue jeans or a black T-shirt and the jeans. I finally wore my favourite Denim blue washed jeans with a Marks and Spencer crisp white shirt and buttoned up the sleeves. I slid on a Tag Heuer wristwatch which had been gifted to me by my mother on my 18th birthday. I sprayed on too much Park Avenue all over my body and was sure I smelled like an exotic spicy vanilla. I put on my favourite pair of brown Woodland boots and looked at myself in the mirror.

I stood in front of the mirror admiring myself, straightening my spikes a bit and practicing different poses. I just hoped I didn't look like a branded showpiece, for I was dressed in branded clothes and items from top to bottom. I thought of toning it down a bit, but then thought it would make a good first impression on Aaruhi. With a last check in the mirror, I was good to go on my first date. My heart was beating fast, my hands were getting cold out of sheer nervousness but my face radiated lots of happiness. I couldn't control my emotions they were overwhelming me. The thought of finally meeting Aaruhi after a month of chatting was making me feel anxious and excited, both at the same time. I kept practising my handshake, what I would tell her or how I would talk to her...there were endless thoughts going on in my mind. At one point, I pinched myself to be sure that this was not a dream. But it wasn't.

I took my car keys, sped out of the house and zoomed away in my little mini sedan. Off to Lake Garden. I took out my mobile and messaged Aaruhi.

Me: On the way...very excited
Aaruhi: Me too :)

I reached Lake Garden and stood at the spot she had told me. It was a nice spot, in the right corner of the garden. It was well-hidden by creepers and short trees. I had been standing there for hardly five minutes when my eyes fell on her.

Like a flower blooming slowly out of a bud, she looked like a dainty flower in the afternoon sun. Her long open hair was swaying in the wind. She was wearing a printed pink skater dress, big hoops and high sandals. She walked like a playful deer, coming closer to me with each step. I couldn't take my eyes off this beauty. My pulse increased again and my feet went numb. My excitement and nervousness knew no bounds.

Finally, she came to where I was standing. She smiled and held out her hand, "Hi Rihen, finally we meet".

"Hi..er...Hi Aaruhi...yes, finally and it's so nice to meet you," I didn't know why I was stammering. I wanted to say a lot but I was totally speechless as she stood in front of me.

As I met her steady gaze, I felt a sudden tremor running through my body. I stared at her rounded face, slightly lighter than ivory with a rose-coloured tint to her cheeks. She had worn a plum shade lipstick on her delicate lips. Her big black eyes were highlighted with thin eyeliner and kajal and her eyes looks very mysterious. Her face sparkled with bliss when she smiled. Her silky lustrous hair fell just past her shoulders. Her knee length pink dress accentuated her curves perfectly and matched the pink hues of her cheeks. She had put on light make-up which illuminated her appearance all the more in the sunny afternoon.

She stood before me like a fairy from heaven, so divinely beautiful...such that she could charm anyone with her drop-dead gorgeous looks.

Our eyes met for a few seconds. I felt an instant magnetic pull towards her. I wanted to hold her...to feel her...but I controlled myself. I didn't want to spoil my first date by making the first move towards her. No, I had to be patient. I couldn't spoil my chances with this damsel standing in front of me who made me go weak in my knees. I knew instantly that she was the first and would be the last girl I would ever love.

10

Somewhere everyone is broken

We walked along a path in the garden...in silence, stealing glimpses at each other. Though we had been chatting on messenger and video calling each other frequently for the past one month, we both were feeling a little awkward meeting for the first time.

"So," we both said together and then stopped, turning to gaze into each other's eyes.

"Uhh, you first Aaruhi," I smiled at her.

"It's nice to finally meet you, Rihen," she said softly.

"Yeah, same here..." I didn't know what else to say at that moment. It seemed that my lips had sealed and words couldn't come out of my mouth.

"What did you tell at home?" I asked her.

"That I'm going out with friends," she said this very casually.

Hmm...I nodded my head.

"And you didn't go to work today?" she enquired.

"I worked half-day...couldn't miss this opportunity," saying this I winked at her.

We kept walking, passing an old canopy of sweet pink and white bougainvillea. The pathway was dusty and laden with fallen leaves and the hot afternoon sun was showering us with its gleaming rays.

"Nice dress, by the way, it suits your skin colour," I told her.
    "Oh thanks," she gave me a mellow smile but I could see her cheeks turning red.
    "You are also looking smart. I like your Tag Heuer wrist watch," she told me in return.

I felt very happy hearing this. She had noticed my love for brands and this pleased me very much. We walked over a narrow wooden bridge and paused to look at the pond below. Five white tiny ducks were waddling smoothly in the water, creating ripples, while the sunlight was casting its golden glistering rays on the water. We look into each other's eyes and she held out her hand to me. Again, a first for me. I held her hand and pressed it lightly. Suddenly, a strong current passed through my whole body and sparked emotions of love in my heart. We stood there on the bridge in silence, holding hands and looking into each other's eyes. I could see a sense of longing in her deep black eyes. Her face had a lot to say. And my heart was open to accept whatever she had to say. I wished for this beautiful moment to last forever.

"So where do we go?" she asked me out of the blue, pulling my hand and dragging me off the bridge.

I didn't want to let go off her just yet. I wanted to keep standing there, holding her hands, staring into her wild eyes, and dream of our lovely future. It seemed as if nature was also showering its blessings on our love. The glistening sun, the warm wind, the colourful flowers, the fluttering butterflies, the calm water of the pond...as if they all were whispering to us...as if they were uniting me and Aaruhi in a bond of love.

She tugged at me again. I pulled her back, but she carried on. Reluctantly, I followed behind her.

"Let's go and sit somewhere so we can talk," she pulled me.

I could see an empty bench under the shade of a big Gulmohar tree. "Let's go and sit there, if that's fine with you?" I nudged her.

"Perfect!" she replied, jabbing me back on my shoulder.

As we approached the quiet spot, I saw a few other couples within our radius. But they were all engrossed in each other. Nobody bothered about their surroundings. They were all so lost among themselves. As we both looked around, we saw that all the other benches were taken. "Well, never mind, we can sit here," saying so Aaruhi made herself comfortable on the granite bench under the shade of the huge tree. Orange petals of the Gulmohar flowers were strewn all over the place. It's a perfect setting, I like it, I was thinking.

After the initial awkwardness, we talked about general things, our daily routine and about our common friends and school life. Once we got into our comfort zone, I asked her the question I had been longing to ask her for a long time. "So, you were going to tell me about your family and something else?"

"Do you really want to know about my past?" she looked at me uncertainly. "It's just...a long and disturbing story. It's too nice a day to spoil with a story of my family, my heartbreak and tragedies. I'll tell you later," she looked at me pleadingly. Then she casually flipped her hair back with her tender hands.

"Uhh...huh..." I cleared my throat, held her soft hands and looked straight into her deep eyes. "I want to know it all...and I am ready to share your pain. Please just let it all out...tell me all that happened."

"Hmm, well then," she said at last.

She cleared her throat, looked up towards the sky and began speaking. I could feel the spasm of her nerves.

"My parents separated when I was very young and my brother was just a baby. Both, my brother and me were left in the care of my Nana and Nani in Navsari. Since then, we have been living with them. Please let me not go into the details of my parents this time." Her voice choked and she was almost on the verge of tears.

"Okay...okay, Aaruhi...please go on...You may share whatever you please and miss out on any details that you don't want to share. I won't mind really," I told her quietly.

Then she continued.

"After I finished my graduation, my Mom had come to visit my Nana and Nani. During that time, they started looking for prospective grooms for me. I wasn't too keen to get married and wanted to study further. However, my parents wished for me to settle down. My mother and father were in touch, though less frequently now. But over matters of our education and now marriage, they had discussed and decided that it was time for me to settle down in life. After rejecting one or two boys initially, my mother got upset with me. She wanted me to choose a suitable groom before she returned to America.

"America?" I interrupted her.

"Will explain this part later," Aaruhi said and continued from where she had left off.

"So, she found an NRI match for me. I was not at all interested. However, on my mother's and Nani's insistence, I met the boy. Our families met at my Nani's home. He was handsome, had a well-paid job in America and quite friendly. But I was a bit apprehensive. He was living in America, a different country, a different lifestyle. Who knows he might even have a girlfriend there, which was quite common. I discussed my apprehensions with my mother who dismissed them all.

My mother told me, 'I know this family well since they also live in America, although a different city. These are genuine people and you will be very happy. It will take time to adjust in the beginning but you will be fine later on. I might even get a chance to visit you once in a while. Don't worry my baby.'

Convinced by my mother, Aditya and I met a second time alone so that we could get to know each other. The second time also we had a good conversation and we both developed a liking for each other. Since he had to go back in 20 days, we got engaged. Everything happened so quickly that I did not have much time to think. But I had developed feelings for him. I even envisioned both of us together, living happily ever after. And he seemed nice so far.

Once we got engaged, his behaviour started changing. He wouldn't respond to my calls properly or even reply to my messages. When I shared my concerns with my mom, she brushed them aside, thinking that I was making excuses. However, this continued for the next few days. Just a day before they had to leave for America, his parents called our family to one of their relative's place where they had been staying. On reaching there, his mother took my mother to another room and discussed something with her. I could hear loud voices with my mother saying "No, this is not right. You should have informed us before" .I could hear soft whispers of his mother... however, I could catch only the word 'sorry' being said repeatedly by her. Both of them came out of the room to where we were sitting.

Aditya came down from upstairs. He took his engagement ring and handed it to my mother. My Mom came towards me and told me, "Aaruhi, take out your engagement ring and give it to me".

"Why?" I asked, utterly shocked by all that was going on.

"Why...what happened?" my Nana-Nani asked my mother. They were totally bewildered by what was going on.

My mother, who was already teary-eyed, couldn't reply. All this while Aditya was standing beside his parents, head bent low.

"What's wrong?" I stood up and went towards my fiancé.

"Aditya...why did you remove the ring?" I shook him hard but he still did not say anything.

"Will someone give me an answer?" I was crying and shaking uncontrollably and unable to understand a thing. My Nana-Nani had got up from the sofa and went towards my Mom who was also crying hysterically now.

Everyone in the house started talking at the same time. There were sound of voices, loud cries and 'sorry' being uttered again and again. Everything was total chaos. And then Aditya silenced everyone. There was pin-drop silence in the house. He first asked my Nana, Nani and mother to sit down. He asked his parents to stand aside. Once everyone had settled a bit, Aditya came to me and held my hand.

He said quietly, "I am sorry, Aaruhi, but I am breaking off our engagement. The reason is that I already have a girlfriend in America. I had informed my parents but they did not approve of her and wanted me to leave her. That is why they brought me to India thinking I would forget about her. I tried hard but I could not move on. You are a nice girl and I got engaged to you on the insistence of my parents. But I just received a call yesterday, my girlfriend back there had tried to commit suicide. Fortunately, she failed to do so and is fine now. But I need to get back to her as soon as possible. I cannot waste any moment. I have booked my tickets for tomorrow, an early morning flight back to America. I told my parents everything and now they too are convinced that I should get married to the one I love. They have agreed to accept my girlfriend. That's why we called you here to inform you about everything. Once again, I am sorry Aaruhi. You are a wonderful girl and I wish you all the best in life. If you could please hand me back that ring. I am sorry again."

Then he became silent again.

I stood rooted to my place, not blinking my eyes. I was unable to breath, and couldn't grasp the situation. It felt as if the whole world had come crashing down on me.

"Sorry? Aditya...you are just sorry? After all the time we spent together? You are only sorry?...Couldn't you have confided in me as a friend? You should have told me before the engagement that you already have a girlfriend. Why me? This is not fair." I shouted at him.

"Aaruhi, please calm down. It is better to be late than never and I said I am sorry," he held my hand.

I pulled my hand out of his and slid his ring off my finger. I threw it at him in anger and walked out from there. He just stood there, his parents besides him, not having said a word till now.

My mother came running after me, shouting my name...but I didn't wait. It was she in the first place who had forced me to meet this guy and get engaged to him. I knew it was not my mother's fault entirely as she did not know about his girlfriend, but I had told my mother about the change in his behaviour and she did not listen to me. She never listened to me anyways.

"Go away Mom, I don't want to hear anything. Please just leave me alone." I shouted at her.

"Look baby, I'm so sorry this happened to you. We know it was not our fault." My mother tried to calm me down.

"Please go. Leave me alone," I said furiously.

My temper was rising with every moment. I had gone red in the face and there was no control over my tongue.

"Aaruhi, this is not the way to speak to your mother," my Nani reprimanded me from behind.

"I don't wish to talk to anyone. All of you, just leave me alone, "saying this, I just went and sat in our car and did not speak to anyone for two days.

My mother went back to America a few days later and we resumed our normal lives. Well, it was never normal for me after that incident.

By the time Aaruhi finished speaking, she was in tears.

11

Our First Kiss

"**S**eriously?" I exclaimed indignantly and she nodded. "But why...?" I asked her. She did not reply.

"Then what happened?" I prompted her.

"Things went wrong. My engagement with Aditya broke up and my whole world came toppling down," she said with tears in her eyes.

"Er...I'm sorry to hear this," I swallowed hard.

There was an expectant silence.

Instinctively, I tilted my head to look at her. After she finished her story, I slowly put my arms around her, hugging her. I was in a blissfully happy state, with her enveloped tenderly in my arms. Maybe I could sit just here like this all afternoon. And we did.

"You know...," she began to say something.

"Sushhh..." I put a finger on her soft warm lips. "Don't say anything as yet". I told her and leaned to kiss her. She hesitated and moved back. I also took a step back and started looking in the opposite direction. Then she suddenly grabbed me by my shoulders, turned my face and kissed me passionately. She held me tight, twirling and forcing her lips into mine. I felt my lips burning, desperately wanting more, to taste every inch of her sweet and salty mouth and to keep holding her. Then as suddenly as she had started, she backed off. Our first kiss lasted for a brief moment but it was nothing short of a dream.

"I like you a lot," she said with a twinkle in her eyes. Then she paused thoughtfully.

My mouth twisted into a smile and I replied, "I love you too".

I felt an explosion of love and emotions burst inside me, which somehow, I managed to hide.

We sat there in silence for a few moments. A small squirrel ran across the bench, stopped and regarded us with two tiny eyes, picked up a nut lying near my foot and then hurriedly scampered off into the hedge.

We sat there for quite some time, hugging each other, holding hands and occasionally kissing each other on the palms and cheeks. The lip kiss didn't happen again, although I desperately wanted one. Both of us didn't realise where the time had gone.

Suddenly three continuous beeps on her mobile distracted us. We slowly released each other's hands. She opened her mobile, read some message and stood up.

"What happened?" I exclaimed.

"I have to leave," she said hurriedly.

"Now, so soon? Why?" I looked at her questioningly.

Our eyes met and I could sense that she was uncomfortable. There was something in her mobile that had distracted her. The romantic mood was totally broken. She seemed in a hurry to go.

"Umm...it was a great afternoon. I had a lovely time. But I have some work and need to go". Aaruhi held my hands.

"So, I'll see you soon then?" I asked with a tiny smile.

"Yes, we will meet soon," saying this she brushed her fingertips over mine before she turned and walked away.

"See you then," I called as she turned to leave.

I watched her walk out of the garden, then turn and head towards the main road till she finally disappeared into the crowd; my whole body still pulsating. I was happy and upset at the same time. This was one of the best days of my life, yet I was upset she had left so abruptly without any explanation. Maybe she did have some work which needed her more than me. But what about my unbearable craving for her!

Back to the Camp

"So, that was our first meeting," I ended my story and looked across at the excited faces of Naira and Karan who were just staring at me.

"Well, so, you have heard my story...now bug off you two," I told them as I stood up to go.

"Not so soon, buddy," Karan told me. He pulled me down again.

"Yes, not so soon, Rihen. And what's the hurry? We still have to spend the evening here. The rain has not stopped." Naira also took Karan's side and insisted that I stay there.

We could still hear the sound of heavy rain outside, and most of the trekkers had either gone to sleep or were busy in their own chit chat.

"Please tell us more. What happened after that? Please Rihen, we want to hear the rest of the story," both of them coaxed me to continue.

Since they didn't leave me with any other option, I continued my story.

"Well, after our first meeting, we both realised that we had desperately fallen for each other. We messaged and talked almost every day on the phone. Our meetings got more frequent. We met at least 2-3 times in a week. She would always make up some excuse at home and come to meet me. We would either meet at the Lake Garden or at some random cafe. The more I talked to her, met her, the more I fell deeply in love with her. She mesmerized me with her talks, her caring nature and her charming personality. Whenever we met, we would kiss passionately, and most of the times she would initiate it. We hugged, we kissed, we would hold hands and talk and talk about our lives, our likes and dislikes and anything and everything.

At times, she would bring food that she had cooked herself. I would buy her expensive gifts every time we met. At first, she would refuse but then she always accepted my gifts. Many times, during our meetings, I observed that she would keep looking at her mobile every now and then and fidget with it, but it did not bother me and I thought nothing of it. Once or twice whenever she received a buzz on her mobile, she left me abruptly without a proper bye or a kiss. She always said there was some important work which I was unaware of. Our romantic meetings and phone calls continued for many months. I was totally in love with her and could do anything for her.

One day, we were sitting at our regular cafe, having our regular cold coffee and pizza. Aaruhi had first brought me to this small and casual cafe which was located in a secluded part of the city. The indoor seating was designed with special corners for couples. After the first few visits, I understood the reason for it. Only couples frequented this shady cafe and most of them were regulars. Once a couple took their seats, the staff wouldn't come around to disturb them. I was a bit surprised as to how Aaruhi had come across this cafe in such a lonely part of the city, but I didn't question her as it was quite comfortable and suited us perfectly. We got a private space where we could hold hands, hug each other and fondle each other without anyone bothering us. Most of the other couples around us also did the same. And no one was bothered about anyone else, even the staff. It seemed a nice, comfortable setting for couples like us. We also became regulars there.

One day, Aaruhi seemed a little upset. After a lot of coaxing, she told me that her mother was unwell and had not been able to send them their monthly expense from America. She had to pay her brother's tuition fees but did not have such a huge amount with her. Her grandparents depended on whatever money her mother would send them. "As you know, my father has never cared about us, forget about taking care of our education or our maintenance". And she burst into tears. I tried to console her but to no avail. She cried and cried for at least another 10 minutes until I could no longer see her like this. I cupped her face in my hands, kissed her forehead, wiped her tears and begged her to stop crying.

"Aaruhi, you don't need to worry, I am here for you," I told her lovingly.

"I know that Rihen, that is why I could relieve my stress and share my troubles with you. I like you a lot," saying this she kissed me passionately on my lips.

"I love you too," I responded amidst her desperate kisses.

"How much money do you require for the tuition fees?" I asked her.

"Of course not Rihen, how can I take money from you like that?" She got very angry with me.

"You say you love me and now you are making me feel like a complete stranger," I told her.

"You are not a stranger to me. You know how much I love you. Look Rihen, I don't want to worry you with my troubles. I was feeling heaviness in my heart for the past so many days due to this stress and I knew only you could lift up my mood. I just told you as I have no one else to share it with. Plus, I knew you are always there for me, so I told you. But it doesn't mean you have to pay our expenses. No way." She was still furious with me.

"Okay fine, you told me so I can ease your worries. So let me just do that. Let me pay for now. You can always pay me back once your mother sends you the money. Is that fine with you? Suits you?" I reprimanded her.

She still didn't look convinced.

I held her hands, and assured her that we should not let money come between our relationship. She was worried about her expenses, and I would just help her out. Then she could pay me back whenever she wanted.

But in my mind, I knew that I would never take back that money. It was just a false promise to her so that she could take the money from me. How could I? I was in love with this girl and could do anything for her. And I was quite well off, so money was never a problem for me.

After thinking for some time, she looked at me and said, "I accept your offer, Rihen. Thank you so much, my darling. I love you. And I will repay this amount as soon as my mother sends us the money". Saying this, she again kissed me hard on the lips, plunging her tongue right into my mouth and after that all worries were forgotten.

I whispered softly, "I just want you and only you. Yes, I know it is madness but love is incomplete without madness".

Aaruhi asserted, "Yes, I know your madness. You drive 100-miles for two hours just to see me for a few seconds. And I love you for that Rihen. I really do". Saying this she lightly kissed me on the cheeks.

Our affair went on for some months, the phone calls and messages were regular but our meetings slowly started reducing. She had taken up a part time job and found it difficult to take out time to come to Surat from Navsari to meet me. However, after that cafe incident, the demand for money consistently increased and I kept giving her money, sometimes small amounts and sometimes large amounts. But this did not affect me in anyway. I was totally in awe of her and would do anything for her. I trusted her completely. Until that one day.

"Hi everyone, get up and get back on track. The rain has stopped. We have to start moving". Suddenly, in the middle of my story we heard Raju Sir's loud voice ordering us to restart our journey to our camping site.

I could see the disappointment on Naira and Karan's faces. But we knew we had to resume our onward journey. We joined the group and followed Raju Sir out of the cave.

Once outside, we gasped in surprise as the dark clouds had disappeared and the sun was glistening through the clear blue sky. We were just a few kilometres from our next camp, which was at DudhuDogh (Dogh means rock cliff). It was getting dark and we all were in a hurry to reach the base camp, so we quickly trekked our way without any stop or hurdle. In about half an hour, we reached DudhuDogh. From there, we were able to see Hamta valley, Deo Tibba, ShirganTungu and its surrounding mountain pastures. It was indeed a sight to behold. We all were awestruck by the beauty of nature. Our camp was ready. We were asked to quickly freshen up, have a quick tea and be ready for the evening adventure activities.

Once we were ready and out on the ground, we saw the set-up at the open ground behind our campsite. A Commando Net Climbing had been setup for other multiple activities. Raju Sir gathered us all in a group while Ching Sir started giving instructions.

"Good evening, everyone! We all have rested enough in the caves. So, now it's time to warm up your body. Get ready for an adventurous evening. As you can all see, we are basically going to do Commando Net Climbing activity followed by a series of other adventure activities. Net climbing is basically a strength building activity, and quite fun. This activity is all about balancing your body weight and climbing up using a net made up of ropes. It is also used as a training activity in many military camps. Commando Net will test your fitness levels through three aspects - **ABC** (Agility, Balance and Coordination). Once you reach the top, you will have to descend through a series of tires arranged on the other side. Next you will do a sky-walk over there," Ching Sir said pointing towards a hanging bridge setup at the far end. "You will be divided into two teams, and whichever team performs both the tasks in less time wins the game. Is that clear?" Ching Sir asked us.

"Yes sir," We all replied with enthusiasm.

We were quickly divided into two teams. This time Naira, Karan, Lakshya and some other boys were in Team A, while

I was placed with Rahul and Naira's girl friends in Team B. We all knew that this activity was going to test our physical strength and started making our own team strategies. Team A went first and we stood on the side to watch how they performed. They formed pairs to do the net climbing and descending down the tires. Naira's friends teased her as we watched her climb slowly and with great effort on the net. She was paired with none other than Karan, who helped her to reach the top of the net. Climbing took time, though coming down was much quicker and easier. As audience, it seemed quite easy to perform these tasks, but when Team A completed the first tasks, they were huffing and panting for breath and seemed exhausted.

When our turn came, we decided to perform the first task in threes. So, I along with two other girls and went first for rope climbing. What seemed easy while standing and watching was not so easy after all. It required hand and leg coordination and agility of our body. In fact, the two girls climbed the net faster than me due to their slim and agile body structure, while I was struggling to climb the ropes and was panting mid-way. The girls waited for me once they reached the top, but I signalled them to carry on and climb down the other side. They showed me a thumbs up and carried on. Tire descending was comparatively easy as we had strong footholds.

The second task, which was Sky Walk, was going to test our flexibility and balance. We could see a built-up of ropes, utility poles, cables, wooden planks attached to each other quite high, literally like walking in the sky.

Ching Sir again gave instructions, "You can all see the set-up at a height and you have to complete the two activities on each side of it- going and coming. There is a hanging bridge at a height of 32 feet with two parallel ropes. You have to cross the bridge with the safety harness connected to you while the guiding rope is controlled by the instructors. Once you reach the bridge, you have to walk on a single rope by holding onto ropes hanging above and move forward to cross it. Again, the team which completes the task in less time will be the winner. This activity improves your balance and team coordination, helps in overcoming obstacles and tests your alertness and sharpness. So teams, get ready to challenge each other at the elevation."

We were all excited with this adventure. It seemed super fun to climb at such a height and do these activities. This time our team, Team B went first. Rahul started the task with one of the boys and both of them did it quite effortlessly. We were cheering loudly for them from below. Next the two girls in our team went. They were in a great hurry to complete the task. They were giggling and doing the tasks very quickly. They both completed the hanging bridge task in less than five minutes. One girl was on the verge of completion but the second girl named Neha, slipped her foot while crossing the single rope. So, she was hanging in mid-air, shouting at us.

Since I was the only member left to do the task, I quickly went up, crossed the hanging bridge with ease and started walking on the single rope. I reached Neha and gave her my hand so she could come back on the rope again. She tried very hard to reach for my hand and at last when she did, she pulled me so hard that even I slipped from the rope and was hanging in mid-air with her. "Sorry, sorry," she was continuously mumbling to me. I gestured to her that it was okay and she should calm down. Time was running out. Our team was supporting us from below, shouting for us to buck up and get going. After hanging for a few minutes, I mustered all my strength and somehow pushed Neha back on the rope. She quickly completed the round and I followed her. We managed to complete the tasks, but we knew a lot of time had been wasted. When we reached to where our team was standing, I could hear them chanting my name for pulling through the activity. Lakshya, though in Team A, came forward and gave me a thump on my shoulder. Out of the corner of my eyes, I saw Naira glancing in my direction, giving me a thumbs up sign. I gave her a slight smile.

Team A went next. They learned a lesson from our team and took each step very cautiously. They did the tasks slowly but steadily and their team also cheered their teammates, continuously motivating them and clapping for them. Team A completed the task without any fault and seemed quite happy.

At the end of both the tasks, the winners were announced. Team B won the Commando Net Climbing task, while Team A won the Sky Walk task. We all were very happy as each team had won one task. We congratulated each other and agreed that the day's adventure activities had indeed been a lot of fun.

Soon, darkness had engulfed the surrounding hills and we could spot a few dots of light here and there in the valley below. We knew the light was coming from the houses of the villagers who stayed nearby. The sun had set, leaving a blanket of black velvet sky with shimmering stars. Everything was just so beautiful. Since it was already late and we had an early start the next morning, we were instructed to quickly have our dinner and get straight to bed. All of us were so tired that we all were fast asleep in our tents before 10 pm.

12

Until Tomorrow

DudhuDogh - Laangha Thach - Sour Tal Lake

The next day, we had to start early, at sharp 7.00 am. Ching Sir had given a brief about the day's trek which involved a steep trail zigzagging through MondruDogh and PhanaiDogh, and then a stopover at Laangha Thach for lunch. Laangha Thach (a balcony) is known as the courtyard of mountain pastures and boasts of magnificent views of lofty mountains and beautiful valleys.

Since we started early, all the members were quite energetic and showed great enthusiasm during the day. We trekked along snowy ridges and enjoyed close view of the Indrasan peaks, Rohtang Pass and the enchanting Beas Kund Massif. Here we were on our way to realising our dreams, as we toiled up step after breathless step, on the final leg of our trek. We had stopping points along the way, during which we were offered noodles and chocolate bars. Once our energy was restored, we carried on with our trek.

The climb then proceeded along a ridge and reached Laangha Thach where we were rewarded by breath-taking views of the surrounding mountain peaks and of the Greater Himalayan range beyond. We stopped for a lunch break which lasted for more than an hour. During lunch time, both Karan and Naira came up to me and continuously bickered at me to continue my story. What happened until that one day? They were very curious I could see but Lakshya was constantly by my side so I couldn't continue with my story then. Later, I winked at them.

From Laangha Thach, we were supposed to reach Sour Tal Lake, but it got quite late so Raju Sir changed the plans. He decided that we should stay overnight at Mahili Thach and visit the Sour Tal Lake in the morning. By late afternoon, we started our enjoyable descent to Mahili Thach camp, glissading at some places on the way. When we finally reached our camp, we were mesmerized by the uninterrupted views of the surrounding Dhauladhar range, Chhota Bhangal, Kaliheyni Pass and the lofty mountain peaks. After a hair-raising trek through the mountains, we breathed easy as we sat in our camp.

Again, we had some adventure activities scheduled for the evening, which we all enjoyed a lot.

This time, Rihen was sharing his tent with Karan, so when everybody had returned to their tents, both of them went out and signalled Naira to join them. She was already standing at the entrance of her tent waiting for them to call her. The trio quickly went behind the campsite, into the woods. They lit a small bonfire. Then Rihen continued his story.

After our meeting the last time, suddenly there was no news from Aaruhi. One day passed, two days and when she didn't call or respond to my messages and calls, I got tensed. What must have happened to her? I checked her social media, but there were no updates. Facebook, Instagram...there was nothing since the past 15 days. My calls were still unreachable. My messages still unanswered. As if she had suddenly disappeared into thin air.

I relentlessly stalked her accounts, looking at her pictures, fondly remembering her. And then it struck me suddenly when I came across the cold face on my screen. The same frown, the screwed eyes and stony expression in most of the pictures.

I had met him only once. He had come to drop Aaruhi at the garden one day. We had a brief exchange of hellos.
"This is Bhaumik, my little brother,"
"And, this is Rihen, my friend."
She introduced us to each other.

The brother and sister were a stark contrast. She, with deep black eyes, fair skin and a mysterious smile had a charming personality. He, on the other hand, had a wheatish complexion, a frown on his forehead and had a stony expression on his face. Her face had something interesting to say and her eyes twinkled with joy. His expressions were cold and his persistent gaze was like that of a tiger stalking his prey. Wearing a blue-collar shirt and black pants, he had put on bright blue glares which made him look like a roadside hero. There was not a hint of warmth when I shook hands with Bhaumik. I could sense his dislike for me.

"Okay sis, I need to rush to my tuitions. Call me when you are free. I will pick you up," Bhaumik told Aaruhi.

"I will drop her at your tuition class. Don't worry." I interjected.

"No need to, I will come by and pick her up," I could sense the resentment in Bhaumik's voice.

Waving goodbye to her, he left without a glance at me.

When there was no news of Aaruhi, I could think of no other option and my mind went back to him. The only plausible person I could think of under the given circumstances. Maybe, I could contact him and try to find out something about the disappearance of his sister. A hundred thoughts were running through my mind at the same time. Will he talk to me? Will he even remember me? What if he has some bad news about Aaruhi?

To do or not to do...I paced up and down the room with heavy steps. My mind was racing. Right now, he was the only point of contact that I could think of. At the end of the day, I finally decided to contact him. It was worth giving a try.

It was 10 pm when I logged into my Facebook account.

I went to messenger. He was online. My heart was beating fast, ready to grasp any news about Aaruhi.

I opened the chat box and sent Bhaumik a 'Hi'. I waited for five minutes. No response. I went out in the balcony to relax my mind. When I came back into the room after another five minutes, there was still no response. I was angry and upset at the same time. He was online, but he hadn't replied to my Hi. I kept on fidgeting with my hair, my clothes, with the things on my desk, to pass my time. But nothing!

I didn't know how to deal with this. You know that someone is online and you wish to talk to them. But when the person doesn't reply or react to your message, it simply means he or she is ignoring you. I was being literally ignored. I couldn't blame him, for we had hardly met and interacted. And even that short interaction had been three months ago. I am not his girlfriend or even a friend for him to remember me.

He was still online.

I wanted to message him again but I just couldn't muster the courage to do so. My fingers got stuck as if I couldn't move them. Being ignored isn't a great feeling. This is what happens in most cases of online messaging. You message a person but he or she does not bother to reply and you are left wondering why.

I couldn't sleep the whole night. That one ray of hope which I had to find Aaruhi had just ignored me. I started recalling any other friends of hers I might know or any mutual contact, a single link to just find her. But nothing came to my overworked mind. The darkness that had engulfed me in the past few days became more dense.

It was 3am when my droopy eyes finally gave in. I went off to sleep and had disturbing dreams. At one instant I was at the Lakeview Garden romancing Aaruhi, the next moment some goons were thrashing me, far away I could see Bhaumik having a good laugh. I murmured in my sleep, not willing to let go of Aaruhi.

Around 5.45 am I woke up from my disturbed sleep. The sun was just rising and casting its rays through the cream sheer curtains in my room. As if it was giving me a ray of hope. I found new motivation.

I sat down again and opened my Facebook account. I went to Messenger and opened the chat box. I typed another message, this time with full conviction. This time the message was a bit longer and more descriptive, explaining who I was.

'Hi Bhaumik,
You might not remember me because we met only once. My name is Rihen, we interacted only for 5-10 minutes when you came to drop your sister at the Lakeview Garden a few months ago. Since the past one week, I have desperately been trying to contact Aaruhi but am unable to do so. Please help me.'
I read the message twice and then hit the 'Send' button.

Now I was anxious, whether he would reply or not. What if he doesn't remember or he doesn't bother to answer? I started fidgeting with anything I could lay my hands on. And then I saw it on the screen. He was online. And to my heart's delight he was typing. Finally, I might get answers to my questions. Something cheered me up. After a week or so my lips curled into a slight smile.

His status showed he was typing and then there was nothing. Then again, he was typing, then un-typing. I waited with bated breath for some answer. The reply came 10 minutes later. It was short and simple.

'Meet me tomorrow at the same garden at 5 pm.'
I was comforted though disappointed. I would have to wait until the next day to get answers to my questions. It was a long shot. I quickly replied to him.
'Why not today? I can't wait for so long.'
He replied,
'I am out for some work and will be arriving back only tomorrow afternoon. And it's just a day...it's not too long. See you tomorrow at 5 pm. Bye.'
And he went offline.

That's it, I thought. So, I have no choice but to wait until tomorrow to get answers to my questions, that too, if he does answer. Otherwise, what if he just calls me up to beat me or gives me a scolding or worse warn me to stay away from his sister. The possibilities were endless. Why didn't he reply earlier and now suddenly why does he want to meet me? Did I miss something? Was it all right to even meet him? Worst case or not it was important to meet him. He was the only link I knew which could lead me to my love. Only he could give me some clues about her unexplainable disappearance. With no other option, I decided it was best to go and meet him tomorrow.

I stayed on Facebook for a little while longer. I started stalking Bhaumik's account, looking at his pictures. There were loads of them. Majority of the photos were with friends. Some Photos from trips, outings and check-ins at different places, all with his gang. He seemed to belong to an all-boy's gang. There were pictures from his travel with friends, most of them looked like hooligans. Then there were several solo pictures of him, those ultra-chic and cool guy photos. Pictures with friends and single model like pictures. As if he really was one. Looking at his photos, it might appear to someone that he was a dashing cool guy, who has so many friends and is socially active. But Aaruhi had always portrayed a different picture of her brother. She mentioned once or twice that her brother was quite repulsive by nature. He hardly liked to go out or make friends and had been an introvert since a small age. I believed her and had never checked his Facebook or tried to get any extra information about him. Today, while browsing through his account for the first time, it seemed he was opposite of what had been portrayed about him. Maybe he wanted to show off on social media, I wondered to myself.

I further scrolled through his timeline and found a few pictures with Aaruhi. I stayed on these for a longer time, wishfully longing for a touch of her warm hands, a slight peck on my cheek from her or a gentle caress down my head and mostly I longed for our passionate kisses.

While looking at his contacts, I clicked on the name 'Urmi Patel' and lo!! had opened their mother's profile. As soon as I did, I found myself staring at a beautiful mixed version of the brother and sister, or rather an older version of Aaruhi. Except that Aaruhi was a bit on the plumper side and her mother had a petite figure. The features were more or less the same, long silky hair, that broad smile, and a pretty face. She too, had deep black eyes but with dark circles under them. I browsed through their mother's account too. She had a few pictures and hardly any info on her profile. She was short and slim and was mostly in western outfits. There were a few old photos of the mother with her kids Aaruhi and Bhaumik in India, and only rare pictures were with her current husband and children. In most of the pictures, she gave her broad grin but her eyes bore a weary expression, as if she was hiding some pain behind that smile. Or maybe it was just her jaded body language behind which was hiding her story.

Both the brother and sister had a difficult childhood. They were very young when their mother left them to marry an Indian settled in America. Bhaumik was just 6-years-old. Aaruhi had never talked much about her step-dad or her step brothers and sisters. She had only mentioned about her mother moving to America when they were quite small.

I wanted to gain as much information as I could about Aaruhi and her estranged family. One thing led to another and I started browsing more through the accounts. I stumbled upon her mother's current husband's account, Aaruhi's step-father. He seemed to be a big businessman in the States. He had uploaded many photos. All the pictures showed him with Aaruhi's mother and two teenage kids, one boy and one girl. From the pictures, it seemed they were his kids, maybe from a previous marriage or from Aaruhi's mother, I didn't know. Again, there were many family pictures, outings and quite a few posts with his lovely wife - Aaruhi's mother. The couple's photos showed how happy she was in that far away land, with her family in the US. She looked very happy.

Aaruhi's father had hardly bothered to take care of them in their mother's absence. Instead, he left his children under the care of their maternal grandparents. He visited them twice a week. And that was it. I had never seen a photo of her father. He did not have any account on Facebook, there was no mention of him anywhere on Aaruhi, Bhaumik or her mother's accounts. He didn't exist on social media. I only knew a bit about him from what Aaruhi had described. He was short, had floppy hair, bulging eyes and droopy shoulders. He did odd jobs here and there to make a living. He barely made enough money to make both ends meet. He struggled with finances and family. Because of less income, the kids grew up with meagre resources. Their family life wasn't good. And maybe that's why their mother left.

Initially, their mother called them every alternate day to inquire about their well-being. But she was far away, too far to hold her children in her loving arms and wrap them in her embrace. The two kids grew up in their grandparent's house without the love of a father or a mother. The frequency of calls from America also declined as they grew older. Their mother had become busy with her life in the States, forgetting about her children in India. She did call them occasionally, on birthdays or festivals or other special days. But that was about it. She came to visit them in India maybe once every two years. The father now visited them once a week. They were deprived of their parents love and this somehow reflected on their behaviour more on Bhaumik than on Aaruhi, I thought. She still seemed mature and was quite jovial, though I did find her mysterious behaviour sometimes. I often felt that she was hiding something from me. But I always overlooked that fact. I was confident about our love, for I had known her in and out for almost a year now. Her brother, on the other hand, seemed very introvert and had an expressionless face, except for the giggles visible in his pictures with his friends or that rare smile when he was posing for his stylish model-like solo photos.

I was still on Facebook when I heard my sister calling me from the kitchen. "Bhai, come have your breakfast. I have made your favourite *KhamanDhokla*. My little sister's voice cheered me up a bit. It was almost 9 am now. I realised I had been on Facebook for more than three hours. Breakfast was a welcome change, so I just shut down my laptop and went towards the dining area.

"Where is Mummy?" I asked when I saw my sister alone in the kitchen.

"She has gone downstairs to get some groceries from the shop", Nisha replied.

"Bhai, what's your plan today?" she gazed at me stealthily.

"Nothing much, why?" I asked while dipping a whole piece of dhokla in chutney. I didn't realize that I was so hungry. By now I had gobbled up half my plate. It was indeed my favourite breakfast.

"Let's go for a movie today," Nisha looked at me pleadingly.

I didn't have much work to do that day, plus I wanted this day to end as quickly as possible so, I instantly said yes to her.

"Great, I will call and book our tickets," she said happily.

"Do we really have to go in a crowd to watch a movie?" I rebuked her.

"Oh bro, I am only inviting three of my friends. That isn't considered a crowd." She gave a jeering look.

"Okay, okay sis, just book the tickets and let me know," I told her with a smile.

We went for the evening show and came home post dinner. The day had passed smoothly without me thinking much about Aaruhi. Thank God for little sisters. They can certainly cheer up any brother's life. Due to lack of sleep from the past so many days and half a day's outing, I just dropped off on my bed and was lost in a long deep sleep.

I woke up late the next day but had almost compensated for my lack of sleep of the past few days. I was suddenly feeling all charged up. I might find out about Aaruhi. Finally, there was some relief for me.

13

A Mysterious Truth

I arrived at the garden at 4.30 p.m. I didn't want to be late. Plus, I was very anxious. I just couldn't stay still at home. I had been fooling around in my veranda most of the morning, hardly ate anything at lunch and kept switching the TV on every now and then to pass the time. Though my sister and mother noticed my absurd behaviour throughout the day but did not ask or say anything to me. The mere thought of meeting Bhaumik was making me nervous. Since it was becoming difficult to pass the time at home, I reached early at the garden.

I looked around the garden, there were very few people that I could see. Some lovebirds could be seen in the nooks and corners, which reminded me of my romantic days with Aaruhi. I strolled around to the places where we used to sit for hours, as if I would somehow find Aaruhi waiting with open arms to embrace me. I stopped at our favourite spot under the blossom of the huge, beautiful Gulmohar tree. I closed my eyes and thought about her. It brought back all the happy loving memories associated with Aaruhi. How we used to sit for hours under the shade of this magnanimous Gulmohar tree in its full bloom in this very garden. Aaruhi loved the bright orange coloured flowers and I used to collect the fallen flowers and hold them together with the stems and broken branches to make a bouquet and present to her. Sometimes, I used to shake the lower branches of the trees so that the Gulmohar flowers fell on her. And then one by one, I would take out the fallen flowers and raw particles settled in her hair. Those moments seemed magical. The holding of hands, the slow caressing of the hair, the slight touch of our lips and...I opened my eyes. I couldn't carry on thinking like this. It hurt me more. I walked off from the spot and went again to the entrance of the garden, where I was supposed to meet Bhaumik.

It was now almost 4.55 pm. I was looking at my watch every other minute. Pacing up and down the garden, I felt like a coiled spring. Yes, I was very very nervous. I didn't know what to expect. Will Bhaumik divulge details about Aaruhi? What if he didn't share her details and just fooled around with me? My mind was continuously whirling with all kinds of thoughts. Then I saw him coming.

He was short and well-built and deeply tanned with intense black eyes. His once black smooth hair now showed bleached brown tips. He had grown a light moustache which made him look like an adult rather than the clean-shaven young boy I had seen last time. He was wearing old jeans and a ripped T-shirt and branded Nike shoes.

His eyes ran doubtfully over me, scanning every inch of me. Unlike him, I appeared in the same state as during my first meeting with him, except for my eyes which had swollen from crying and lack of sleep over the past few days. I was wearing a simple grey round neck T-shirt with black jeans and grey sneakers. My head was all fuzzy and my heart was pumping loudly. Every inch of my skin was pricking under his razor sharp stare.

"Hi," he said at last. "Rihen, Right?" He held out his hand.

"Er..yes, I'm Rihen, Hi Bhaumik. Nice to see you" I shook his hand. His skin was hard and rough, just like a piece of tree bark. On the other hand, I was as numb and cold as ice.

"You wanted to talk about my sister?" he looked at me questioningly.

"Er...yes," I replied. I don't know why I was stammering.

We walked towards a bench in the park. I couldn't help noticing how different he looked from his sister. He took long strides and casually went and sat down on a bench, offering me to sit next to him.

"So, tell me what is it?"Bhaumik asked.

I looked at him uncertainly. "I wanted to know about Aaruhi. She is not responding to my messages and calls and I don't know how to contact her or what happened to her. I could think of no one except you. So, out of desperation and worry I got in touch with you," I told him, explaining why I had contacted him.

He produced his phone, opened his Facebook and showed me a list of Aaruhi's friends on Facebook. Most of them were boys. He opened messenger and showed me the messages exchanged between Aaruhi and other guys. They were all similar, just like she used to message me. And not just to one but multiple guys.

I felt a jolt of shock. 'Aaruhi? But she loved me so much? Or was she pretending all along?'

"Hey buddy, don't be so surprised,"Bhaumik nudged me.

"Huh," I swallow hard. I couldn't speak a word.

"I thought you must have guessed from her behaviour and not have taken her too seriously,"Bhaumik looked at me. He gave a small frown. "I don't know what she told you, but I know for sure that after her engagement broke, all her relations were just a fling to mend her broken heart. She has never really been in love with anyone." He said at last.

I sat there, frozen, staring at the dust on the ground. It couldn't be...There must be something wrong. There must be a mistake. Her brother might not know about our relationship. Aaruhi could not possibly do this to me. No. I refused to believe it.

I closed my eyes, trying to calm down. But I couldn't think straight. All our conversations, our sweet talks, the promises of love passed in front of my eyes that beautiful romantic days spent in this same park it all came back to me.

At last, I opened my eyes and looked at the messages still open on Bhaumik's phone. My happiness had suddenly vanished. There was a kind of iciness around my heart. I was desperately trying to remember if Aaruhi had mentioned anything about other boys or her friends or about not liking me. Her behaviour did seem odd sometimes but overall, she always exhibited her profound liking for me. And I trusted her all this time.

Oh God!

I leafed through the messages one more time, desperately searching for some indication that this was not Aaruhi. This might be someone else. Or maybe Bhaumik was making all this up. He doesn't like me and might be trying to put up this false story so that we both get separated. All kinds of thoughts were rushing through my mind. My heart still wanted to trust her. My brain was asking me to be practical and accept the truth. As I scrolled through the messages, I felt dizzy. 'Why did this happen to us or to me? What wrong had I done? What should I do now? I buried my head in my hands. I had fallen head over heels in love with Aaruhi. She had become my world. She meant everything to me. Now suddenly her brother comes and tells me it was all a lie. The whole relationship has no meaning at all. Aaruhi doesn't love just me, she loves no one and is just messing with the feelings of everyone.

Bhaumik put a hand on my shoulder and whispered, "It will be okay, you just have to accept the truth and move on. My sister will never meet you again and has gone from your life for good. Just like she does with every other boy she meets. You were just a target. And now she will be looking for another one. I have showed you the proof. Now forget Aaruhi. There was no love, only lies. I knew she tricked you the moment you messaged me about wanting to meet me. I only agreed to come and meet you today to tell you the truth and get the situation straight. I'm sorry on behalf of my sister. But there's nothing more I can do to help you. Time will heal everything. The sooner you accept the truth, the better it will be for you. Forget Aaruhi."

Forget Aaruhi...But, how could I tell him that just the thought of it fills me with horror. How can I just forget her? For an instant I felt as though I didn't know what Bhaumik was talking about. My world had come crashing down and I didn't know what to do about it. Aaruhi had been unfaithful to me. And that was the end of my love life.

For a few moments I couldn't speak. I couldn't even think properly. Without knowing what I was doing, I walked away from Bhaumik and went straight home.

At home, I tried to keep calm, but a wave of sorrow was ripping through my whole body. I had made a mistake in understanding Aaruhi and now I had to face it. For days I just sat in my room, staring into nothingness. My surroundings seemed to shrink. I didn't feel thirsty or hungry. Sometimes I picked up my phone and dialled her number. But it repeatedly said 'the number you have dialled does not exist'. I put down the phone, shaking all over. My last attempt to talk to her once more obviously didn't work. I felt like I was hallucinating.

I had made a big mistake.

I wanted to run away somewhere. Run away from everything.

I don't understand how it happened. I don't understand anything at all. I sometimes wondered if it is all a bad dream and I will wake up and Aaruhi will be with me, in my loving arms. I kept hoping that she might call me sometime, apologise for her act and come back to me. But this was not the truth. The reality was that she had cheated on me. She was never going to come back. My breath started getting shorter and my head started reeling. I sat near the window of my room and looked up at the clear blue sky to feel better.

But I did not feel better. I felt worse.

Suddenly I jumped up in panic as the door of my room opened and my sister popped in. "We are waiting for you to come have lunch with us. By the way, what's the matter? You seem upset about something".

I didn't feel like talking to her right then. In fact, I don't feel like talking to anybody at all. My head was hurting so much, I had no idea what my sister was saying.

"Are you alright?" She peered at me. "You look terrible!"

"Nothing, I just have a terrible headache," I replied.

A moment later, she came to me and took my hand, dragging me downstairs for lunch.

"Bhai, just eat the yummy khichdi and kadhi Mum has made. Your headache will vanish in a jiffy," she was muttering while dragging me down.

Months passed. I lost count of the days and nights. Aaruhi had cheated on me. It was like a drum constantly beating in my head. I was still not able to digest the fact that she had left me. I didn't understand anything of why it happened.

My mind kept going over everything again and again. Over and over, obsessively thinking about Aaruhi, our conversations and the many love promises. And today, she has left me, just like that without any warning, without any goodbyes, without reason, without explanation, she cheated on me. Cheated on so many other guys, who knows! How could I have not seen?...How could I have overlooked? How could I have not realised anything? That constant looking on the mobile phone, always active on her Facebook account, the abrupt goodbyes whenever we met. How could I have not figure it out then? I had a constant urge to delete all my info and photos from my Facebook account, to get off social media completely. I opened my account many times but always backed off at the last moment. There was still a tiny hope that maybe I might see her online someday again. Maybe I could demand an explanation from her for doing this to me.

I started going for work. I went for work, came back home, ate, slept and repeated this routine automatically every single day. My parents and sister coaxed me and tried to talk to understand what had happened, what was wrong with me. But I just excused it as work stress.

One day, barely knowing what I was doing, I got up from my bed and opened my laptop. I booked a ticket for the first trekking date available on the site. Once the booking was done, I felt a relief. I knew for sure that I had to get out of there. I needed to go away from there. I needed to go far away.

I packed my bags and informed my parents and sister about where I was going. Nobody questioned me or protested about my decision. Knowing I wasn't in the best of moods since the past so many days, they just let me be. Mum kissed me goodbye. I left my house with my rucksack and walked towards the auto stand. Fifteen minutes later, I got down from the auto and walked through the crowded railway station as if I was on auto-pilot mode. I climbed up the stairs and kept walking. My mind was still hurting, my legs were aching. Somehow, I managed to reach the platform. I finally slowed down and came to a halt near an empty bench. And that's how I came to this trekking trip.

> *All the problems are of the Heart*
> *And the Heart is not always right*

14

Sour Tal Lake

Why do we love so deep?
To the person who is not in our destiny?
I wish we had a remote control
So we could switch on or off our feelings.

"So, here I am now. Sitting in front of you," saying this, I finished my story.

By the time I ended my story, Karan and Naira were staring hard at me.

"Are you crazy? How could you not know? I mean common Rihen..." Karan was shaking me hard.

They say love is blind. Truly, I couldn't think of anything else but her. I couldn't see the care of my family and friends but kept missing her innocent face. Her deep brown eyes, her chubby smile, it all came in front of me. I felt her caressing my rough palms, then slowly rubbing the tears from my eyes. She was there. And in a blink, she was gone. As days dragged by, my hopes had started falling. But I still held on to her. Her love promises still rang in my mind. And here I was sitting in front of my two friends trying to justify what had happened.

"As I told you guys, she had a difficult childhood, a very odd one to believe. Maybe it might have taken a toll on her emotionally for all these years. One never knows."

"Rihen, stop acting so stupid. How can you let it happen?" Naira sounded shocked.

"Why the hell don't you accept that her love was fake. I mean, Rihen…" Naira was furious.

"Well, I do know!" And I felt tears streaming down my face.

"Hey, hey, hey…look it's okay. Please don't cry. We are your real friends and we are here for you. We are sure time will heal everything and you'll forget about her." They motivated me with a lot of positive talk.

But even as I felt my spirits lifting, I knew I was like some lonely traveller, desperately looking at a mirage in the desert. Suddenly Naira and Karan came towards me and gave me a tight hug. It was definitely a warm group hug and calmed me a bit.

Naira held my hand and said, "Rihen, your smile is a signature of your personality, do not allow it to be washed away by your tears or be erased by your anger. Life is tough, take every step carefully."

"Okay guys, we need to go to sleep now. See you in the morning," I said.

"Goodnight Rihen," Karan let go of me and shook my hand.

"Goodnight Rihen, take care," saying this Naira patted me on the cheek.

All of us went towards our tents. When I reached mine, Lakshya was already snoring loudly. I dozed off as soon as I lay down in my sleeping bag. That night, however, I had nightmares and couldn't sleep well. I kept tossing and turning in my bed, dreaming about Aaruhi and myself. I was running in a big garden aimlessly calling out for Aaruhi but couldn't see her anywhere. I went from one place to the next searching for her but I could only see glimpses of her face, her hair or she holding out her hand and suddenly she was running away from me.

'Aaruhi...come back...please come back to me. Where are you? I miss you...Aaruhi...' and I was shaking. When I opened my eyes, Lakshya was standing with a glass of water ready to splash it on me.

"Oh no no...wait, don't splash water on me. I am already awake," I said laughingly to Lakshya.

"Okay buddy, but you need to get ready fast. You are late, everyone else has already started their breakfast and packed their bags. Common friend, hurry up," saying this he went out of the tent.

I quickly packed my things, brushed and just splashed water on my face. As soon as I was ready, I went out to have my breakfast. It was freezing cold outside. Everyone was packed in their warm furry coats and woollen hats and boots. I also put on my jacket and fleece gloves. Naira was dressed in a light pink long fur overcoat and big boots. She had put on a white and pink woolly and was looking very cute. Her cheeks were rosy due to the cold and her lips bore a strawberry colour. I couldn't help but stare at her. Breakfast was hot parathas, tea/coffee and boiled celery Momos with chutney. After breakfast, we all lined up outside our tents with Raju Sir and Ching Sir giving us the usual instructions.

"Today, we are off to our final destination - Sour Tal Lake... and we promise that it will be one of the best experiences of your life...something which many of you will never have encountered before. So, get ready team, and let's start our ascent.'

Everyone was as excited as on the first day of our trek. With high excitement, came the realisation that our trip was finally coming to an end. But we didn't want to spoil our mood, so we all geared up for the final and strenuous trek ahead of us. From our campsite, we were told that our ascent would be quite stiff. Our trail would proceed along a long snowy slanted ridge towards Sour Tal Frozen Lake (3,700 m). As we walked slowly along the snowy ridge, we had amazing panoramic views of Deo-Tibba Massif, Inderkilla, Indrasan peaks, Rohtang Pass, and the enchanting mountain peak of the Beas Kund Massif. The sun was shining brightly overhead, but chilly winds were blowing.

About an hour and a half into our journey filled with excitement and hard walk, we stopped near a small wooden bridge for our first break. I was feeling a little light-headed. My eyes were a bit puffy from lack of sleep. Others in the group too, were breathing heavily and were slightly dizzy. Maybe it was the altitude or the steep trek which was giving us a little rough time. Everyone around me were chattering loudly, clicking pictures and enjoying themselves to the fullest. Even Naira, Karan and I clicked photos together. Although they tried to cheer me up during the trek, I was still not in the best of moods. But I knew that our time together was coming to an end and I should enjoy these little moments than think about my past. I regained my composure and went towards the group, clicking pictures with other team members and even Raju Sir and Ching Sir.

Soon we started climbing again. At 13,700 feet, the Pass had been freezing and we stopped quite often to wrap ourselves. During the journey we gratefully accepted the hot cups of ginger tea. The cold winds were making us numb. We walked on scattered snowy and grassy patches right up to the top of Sour Tal Lake. The roads were not the best, but the bare mountainside, the luscious forest and excellent food more than made up for it.

Naira, Karan and I walked the final mile to the lake, taking in each sight with awe. The small glacial lake formed in the depression was mostly frozen but there was beautiful scenery all around it. Every one of us was mesmerized by the spectacular sight that surrounded us. It was a huge lake right at the top of the mountain, and it was really very chilly. With many crevasses around, I carefully jumped from stone to stone. The three of us trudged along making our way through the stones and the frozen water, gradually losing all sense of time. At Sour Tal Lake, breath-taking scenery surrounded us on all sides. We appeared to be tiny elements amidst this vast frozen lake.

Our group slowly walked away from the lake into the realm of the high mountains, the mystic glaciers and the serene lake. Together, nature formed a vast stillness, creating euphoria for all of us. Finally, we stopped at one end of the Sour Tal Lake, nestled amid mountains at an altitude of 4,200m. Most of the folks went down to the lake, while some of us stayed back. We had time on our hands as we had to return to the camp only by evening. When we were served lunch, sitting near the Sour Tal Lake everything seemed so surreal. Our trekking group was enjoying hot delicious food along with a view of blue frozen water, snow-capped mountains and open skies. I felt a feeling of triumph, a feeling of joy, a feeling of fulfilment while sitting at this height overlooking the mesmerizing view.

"What a beautiful view," Naira exclaimed.

After lunch, we all played a game. After the game was over, Raju Sir gave us half an hour to do whatever we wanted. He told us to assemble at 6 pm near the lake. As soon as he announced this, Naira grabbed my hand and pulled me behind her.

"What is it Naira?" I asked as I was surprised when she pulled me.
"Come on, come with me," she whispered.

"But where?" I was still bewildered. I hadn't even put on my jacket or cap. "Wait, let me bring my jacket at least," I said and started to move to where I had kept my jacket.

But she pulled me even harder.

"Come on now Rihen, it's not so cold," saying this she literally dragged me with her.

I had no option but to follow her majesty's command. I went along with her to wherever she was taking me. And off we went, just the two of us, on top of a hill.

15

The Proposal

"Maybe this is what heaven looks like," Naira broke off the eerie silence between us.

"Yes, I am sure." I finally smiled, a smile which came straight from the heart, pure, raw and innocent. I looked right into her eyes.

We were standing atop a hill, with the majestic snow-capped Himalayas looking down at us, the deep valleys and the mesmerizing scenery in front of us. It did look like a dream sequence.

Naira caught my hand. Of course, we both were wearing gloves, so our hands didn't touch but I felt a spark within me. We kept standing there in silence for a few minutes, content with our hands clasped together.

"None of us would have ever dreamt about this. Isn't it Rihen? It is so beautiful," she said softly, looking into my eyes.

"Yes, it is," I agreed.

"I want to tell you something, so close your eyes." Naira told me.

"What is it?" I became anxious.

"Just close your eyes, will you?" she pleaded.

"But why?" I did not give in easily.

"Will you just do as I say Rihen, just for two minutes," Naira again begged me.

"Okay, fine, whatever you say," I replied and closed my eyes. Try as I might, but I couldn't hear a sound and kept wondering what she was doing. After two minutes she asked me to open my eyes.

When I opened my eyes, I saw her kneeling in front of me, with one hand outstretched towards me and one hand behind her back. Her pink fur jacket made her cheeks look even more pink. Her long brown hair was fluttering in the wind with strands brushing her face. She moved the strands from off her face but they still kept coming back. She held a heart made out of snow in her hand.

I was a bit confused and didn't know what to do or how to react. I just stood still staring down at her.

"I love you, Rihu, and I want to be a part of you. I am giving you my heart," saying this Naira forwarded the snow-covered heart to me.

My feet were stuck to the ground and I did not move an inch. My face was blank and I had no expression. Suddenly I started feeling dizzy.

Her eyes expressed her emotions. She again said, "Rihu I want to spend the rest of my life with you".

I was absolutely dumbfounded. I couldn't speak. I couldn't even bring myself to lift a hand to take the snow heart which was now melting in her hand. I had lost all track of time or day or where I was standing. I seemed to have lost all senses. I felt totally disoriented.

"Rihu ...my Rihu, I'm waiting ..." whispered Naira.

I heard my name being called Rihu for the first time. And then I realised that she was still on her knees in front of me, grasping the last of the melted snow heart. I moved towards her and pulled her to her feet.

"Naira, I really don't have words to say anything right now. I mean...you...like this...for me..." I was stammering. Then, I took a hold of myself.

"Look." I turned to face her in the warm sunlight, my heart pumping. "I also like you a lot and you mean a lot to me".

"Then what is the problem? Or who is the problem? Aaruhi right...," she said angrily.

"Yes and no. I don't want to talk about her but I also can't get her out of my mind. I hate myself for wasting my time and words over a girl who didn't value me. But I am not the right guy for you. I am not in the right state of mind to give you the love you deserve. You deserve someone better than me, more than me. Naira, I cannot accept your proposal. I am sorry if this hurts you, but I have no choice," I told her gently as I didn't want to hurt her.

Naira listened in silence. She did not plead, nor did she repeat what she had said. Her face became sullen, shadowed in the winter sun, and I couldn't tell what she was thinking.

"I'm sorry," I pleaded guiltily. "I just don't want to ruin your life...you know...I'm sorry Naira. I can't be with you," was all I could utter.

"Why not?" she retorted and I could hear the hurt in her voice. "You don't love me?" she asked, looking straight into my eyes.

"No!" I said in dismay. "Of course I like you and I trust you! If it had been anything else..." I broke off. "Naira, you have to understand. I have told you all about my past. I am still recovering from one shock. It has not been easy for me. I like you a lot but I don't love you. Love doesn't exist for me anymore. It is not for me. Rather, I'm not for it. I am not yet ready to fall in love again," I put forth my point. There was a feeling of despair inside me. Maybe I had ruined everything? Maybe I should have requested some time to think over her proposal?

For a while, Naira said nothing. She just stared down at the lump of melted snow which had been in the shape of a heart some minutes ago.

"I'm happy the way we are. I just want everything to stay the same." I ended the conversation. She just nodded.

"Okay, let's go," saying this she turned and started walking.

We walked again through the snowy path towards our camp. Neither of us said a word. There was no sound except for our footsteps on the rough hilly road and a distant bird hooting. I felt an aching pain inside my body. We had almost reached the camp. She looked towards me silently, her expression almost grave. I could feel my breath thickening. I met her gaze and saw tears welling up in those innocent eyes. But before I could wipe them, she ran towards the camp.

That night I couldn't sleep. I tried to close my eyes, trying to ignore the stab of pain inside me. But it just wouldn't go. I tried to recollect the morning scene again and again in my head, and was on the verge of crying. The whole night I kept thinking about Aaruhi, Naira and myself. This wasn't the way things were supposed to be. Not with Naira. She was different. She was innocent. She had supported me and stood by me. Instead, now we would be apart. She might not even look at me. I tossed and turned in my bed till it was 4 am, when I finally fell asleep.

The next morning, when I met Naira, she smiled at me. I was relieved. At least she had smiled. I hadn't expected her to even look at me. By evening, she seemed a bit normal and even said 'Hi' to me. So, we certainly were still friends.

"Naira," I went up to her during lunch and tried to start a conversation.
"Rihen, I'm fine. And we are still friends," saying this she pulled my cheeks, smiled and went to have lunch with her friends.

I heaved a sigh of relief. At least things were normal between us. She was so simple and so understanding. She didn't expect anything at all from me. And she had accepted me with all my strengths and weaknesses.

After our last visit to the frozen Sour Tal Lake, it was the end of our trekking adventure. After days of sheltering in the embrace of the snowy mountains, our trekking had been completed. We were headed back to our base camp at Prini. We were exhausted, happy and nostalgic all at the same time. As our group started the descent, a flock of sheep crossed our path. They looked at us, wondering why we were leaving such an ideal place.

Honestly, we all had a good time during the entire trekking trip. The course of the trek had been very interesting. Walking for four to six hours every day, we experienced hardship as well as the thrill of climbing the mountains, reaching our destination and exploring the woods. Yes, the latter half of the days were reserved for games or some sort of team recreational activities. But the things we would miss the most were playing pranks with each other, the dining together, the tent time and so much more. Between meals, the adventures of the day were discussed. And our meals were always so delicious and healthy - generous breakfast spreads to hot, piping dinners. A hot plate of noodles and a cup of tea/coffee had become a routine. Imagine enjoying the food with a view of the deep valleys, snow-capped mountains and starry skies. We had lived this life for the past few days, trailing through the thick pine forests, alpine meadows, Garhwal villages and snow - a setting so surreal that we will miss all this in our daily life.

There had been difficult times also. There were days when we toiled up, step after breathless step, spent restless nights in the tents and were totally exhausted. There were times when our knees were fine, but our thighs used to protest strongly; when the leg couldn't take another step; when we felt so tired that we couldn't sleep. During those tough moments, when we stopped to look at the scene around us, all our tiredness would melt away. It would simply vanish. As if nature was working its wonders on us. The tantalising views of the snow-capped peaks, the glistening sunrise and the ethereal sunsets, the night sky full of stars, the chirping of the birds, the rustling of the leaves, the gurgling of the small water streams and the playfulness of the village children - it was nothing but a lifetime of experiences that we would take back with us, moments that we would cherish forever.

And for me, it had been a life-changing experience. When I had begun this trip, I was full of doubts, mistrust, apprehension and frustration. I had begun to lose faith in life. But these feelings had changed to some extent during this trip, when I met Naira, a cute and innocent girl. And then I developed a bond with Karan who became a good buddy. Slowly, they put faith back into me. And Naira, what do I say about her? She was like an angel from the mountains just to put my life back together. She brought stability and security in my life. I had gradually begun to trust someone after a long long time.

On the last day, at the Prini Base Camp, we had a bonfire party from 6 pm onwards. Everyone was excited. It was a mark of celebration of the successful end of our trekking trip and the beginning of a new journey. Ching Sir had already lit the bonfire. He had also invited some locals to join us. The villagers, dressed in their native attire, had arrived in a huge group and were chattering in their local language. Many of the members started assembling outside. It was getting dark.

I was standing there with Karan, waiting for Naira to join us. Soon she came out with her friends. Karan waved over to her. She waved back and signalled to him that she would join in some time. After some light snacks, we all sat down around the bonfire. Naira joined me and Karan.

"Hi Karan," Naira came and hugged him.

"Hi Rihen," Naira slightly brushed my shoulders.

"Common let's go and take our seats or we will miss the fun," Karan mumbled.

We sat with the rest of the group. Ching Sir, Raju Sir and the other staff members were sitting together. The locals were sitting at the opposite end on one side. The circle was complete. The bonfire was fully lit by now. The stars had come out in huge numbers and looked like diamonds in the vast black sky. A chilly wind was blowing and we all hugged our leather jackets and furry coats close to our bodies. Many of them had even brought their shawls and blankets to keep warm. It was a mesmerizing night.

The program started with the villagers singing their traditional folk songs. The tune was so soothing and their voices so melodious that we all fell into a trance. Each song had its own uniqueness, its own story line and emotions, its own melody. We felt so happy and relaxed listening to the pahari songs. It soothed her hearts and soul. When the beats got fast, many of us stood up to dance. It motivated the locals and they sang more merrily and loudly. All of us thoroughly enjoyed the traditional folk songs and dance. Then we played the game of dumb charades, which turned out to be quite interesting.

The teams were divided and Naira and I were in opposite teams. The game started some were quite serious about the acting, while some were so funny, making us all laugh. One of my team members gave Naira the famous movie 'Sholay' and she acted so well that her teammates guessed the movie's name within a minute.

When it was my turn for acting, Naira came from their team to tell me the name of the film on which I had to act. She came forward to whisper in my ears the film's name. Her face was inches away from mine. For a second, I wanted to kiss her but controlled my urge. I was overjoyed. I sensed that even she was elated. I held her in my arms for a few seconds. I could sense that people around us were observing, so I reluctantly let her go.

But Naira again came forward to tell me the name of the film.

"Okay Rihen, the name for your film is Chokher Bali," she whispered softly in my ears.

"Sorry what, I didn't understand," I tried to act innocent as I wanted her to stay as close to me for some more seconds.

"Cho... what?" I went near her and asked again.

"Huh...huh...Chokher Bali," she whispered a bit loudly in my ear. Her hands touched my cheeks. I felt a spark within me. It was unlike the previous one I had felt whenever I was with Aaruhi.

I had no clue about the movie or the name given to me. I felt lost. But my teammates were motivating me, chanting my name loudly as if that would help them guess the movie. I tried to act as natural as I could, trying to break the movie name into half, trying to act on the word 'Bali,' and so on. Five minutes passed and my team members still had no clue about the movie. I could see Naira laughing at me. When I revealed the name, it seems no one had ever heard that movie name and pardoned me for not acting well.

After the games, we all had a hearty *pahadi* dinner. Just when the dinner was being served, Raju Sir had some work in the staff tent and called me there. Fifteen minutes later, I came out of the tent and was just crossing over to another tent when I heard two familiar voices. At first, I was surprised to hear them talking like this. I stood still and overheard their conversation.

"Yes, I had a crush on a girl. But it was only attraction and not Love. At that time I was learning photography in the studio and she was the pretty receptionist there. She was a simple homely girl. One day I was sick and did not go to the studio. So, she messaged me that Sir was asking about my absence. I replied that I would not be coming to the studio as I was not well. From that day on, we chatted frequently and started meeting regularly. Most of the time when we met, she would pose in different angles and I would click her pictures. She would upload her photos on social media and her followers increased day by day. All the while I captured all her photos and supported her to gain popularity in her professional journey. She garnered a lot of attention on social media and slowly turned into a blogger. I then fell in love with her and proposed to her. I will never forget what she told me that day because I never expected such a response from her.

She said "Are you mad? Look at me and look at yourself. I'm a famous blogger and you are just a novice photographer. Do you really think I would choose someone as cheeky as you? I am stylish and super glamorous and you...you are an average guy who has nothing special. How did you even think that I would say yes to a lanky guy like you?"

"After this we broke contact with each other. And I lost trust on girls. But this was before I met you Naira. You are totally different. I have been observing you from day one. You are special. You care for others. You are not selfish. You are beautiful inside out and I think we would make a great pair." Naira did not reply but just stood there, listening to Karan.

I did not want to listen to their conversation anymore and just moved away from there. But a thought occurred to me, about what Karan had just said. Maybe they both were perfect for each other.

Later, that night, there was a surprise for us. A DJ system was specially arranged for us to dance the night away. After the party ended, we were all exhausted but there was one final thing to do, without which the whole program would have been incomplete. All the group members decided to give a vote of gratitude to the whole trekking team.

We thanked Ching Sir, Raju Sir for their immense support throughout the trip and their flawless management. Then we thanked all the staff members who had handled the arrangements of the trek because it was due to their efforts that everything had gone so smoothly. Many of us hugged the cooks, support staff and other trekkers with a silent assurance of meeting them again for yet another trek. Members shook hands with each other too. We all got very emotional. It was a teary moment as everyone bid goodbye to everyone.

Karan Naira and I stole a moment away from the crowd for ourselves. The three of us had a group hug. After that Karan went to meet his other friends, I was left alone with Naira.

"Naira..." I said, "Please don't mind my behaviour yesterday. I'm sorry if I hurt you."

"Yes, I'm hurt Rihen, and I don't know why you don't trust me," she said frankly.

"It is not about trust, please Naira, but..." I stopped midway.

"I can understand Rihen, but I won't stop trying," she told me looking straight into my eyes.

"I am certain of my decision," I told her determinedly.

"We will see," saying this she held my hand. "Whatever happens, but we will remain friends forever."

I agreed whole heartedly with this.

We then went back to our tents.

Maybe this is not the end, but the beginning of something.

16

Daily Casual Meets

The harsh crackling sound woke me up from my deep slumber. I picked up the alarm clock and pressed the stop button. It was 7.15 am. There's still time, I thought. I could hear the whistle of the pressure cooker from the kitchen and rock music playing from my sister's bedroom. Only she could listen to rock so early in the morning. Feeling lazy to get up, I pulled back the blanket over my face and went off to sleep again.

When I woke up next, it was 8.45 am. Oh no! I'm late...I'm going to miss the train. I hurriedly scrambled out of bed, brushed my teeth and had a quick shower. I dressed up shabbily and just pushed back the strands of hair falling on my face. I wish I had a few more minutes to at least comb my hair or stare at myself in the mirror, but I didn't. I took my mobile and wallet and rushed out of my bedroom.

"Rihen, breakfast is ready." My mother shouted from the kitchen. I gulped down some biscuits and tea and, in my hurry, I spilled some tea on my pants.

'Oh no,' I moaned but continued walking towards the door.

"At least change your pants and go Rihen," my mother called out.

"Not now Ma, I am late. See you later." I replied to her.

Indeed, there was not a minute to be lost.

I started my car and zoomed off towards the railway station. It seemed as if all the traffic was on my route. I got frustrated as I shuffled through the heavy traffic. When I finally reached the station, I could not spot her. I checked my watch twice, and knew I was late by 15 minutes. I walked along here and there, my eyes frantically searching for her.

"You're late," I heard a voice behind me.

I swivelled around in delight to see Naira standing right behind me, looking absolutely stunning in a pastel coloured salwar kameez. Her kohl filled eyes twinkled distinctly.

"Er....yes, I know I'm a little late," I replied, my hands glued to the spot where I had spilled tea on my pants.

"Not a little late, huh," She smirked at me. "By the way, nice to see you again," she offered her hand.

"Same here Naira." I glanced at her and hastily brought out my hand to shake hers and greeted her with a quick hug. Both of us smiled at each other.

"Hang on. You seemed to have gained a lot of weight," she observed, looking me up and down.

"Let's go," I said trying to ignore her comment. I picked up her bags and reached for my car keys.

Okay, maybe I had gained a little weight since I had come back from the camping trip.

Naira wanted to pursue a short-term course in Fashion Designing and had chosen Surat to do so, citing it to be the city of textiles and fashion. Or maybe it was just an excuse. She really wanted to be with me. However, this is what I thought. God knows what the truth was. Nevertheless, the very fact that she was going to be in my city rose my excitement levels. I was happy that we would be able to spend some more time together.

She had booked a room in the girl's hostel near her college campus. Her classes were from 11 am till 6 pm, after which she was generally free. This gave us a lot of time to meet, interact and get to know each other. We often met outside her college or her hostel or sometimes we went to the cafes close by or just went for quick bike rides. Our bond was growing stronger by the day. I didn't feel sad anymore. The days which had seemed to just drag by previously, now turned into hopes for something new and exciting with Naira.

The constant buzzing sound of my mobile woke me. It was 6 am. Wondering who would be calling me at this hour, I swiped my mobile and saw three missed calls from Naira. Before I could think further, my phone started ringing again.

"Hi Naira, good morning," I said sleepily.

"Good morning Rihen," she replied enthusiastically. "Get ready, I'm coming to pick you up."

"Hmm…okay," I replied sleepily.

"What hmm...wake up, sleepy head. I will be outside your house in 10-15 minutes. So, you better wake up." She said laughingly.

"But where are we going?" I sounded disinterested.

"I have a surprise for you." I could hear a giggle on the other end of the line.

"Surprise, at this hour? So early on a winter morning?" I was put off at the thought of snuggling out of my warm blanket and going out in the chilly morning to who knows where.

"I hope you are not taking me to the garden for an early morning walk? I will not talk to you if you did that. Why don't you come home and make me a coffee and we can have it comfortably in my room?" I was adamant about not going out.

And she was equally stubborn about taking me out for the surprise.

"Okay. I will get ready," I finally gave in to her request grudgingly.

Half an hour later, we were standing in front of the city's one of the top gyms. Body Build was a reputed gym and always bursting with fitness freaks.

"Whoaa...what are we doing here at this time?" I was indeed surprised that at 6.30 in the morning we were standing outside a gym.

"Wait...did you join here and came to show me your workout?" Haha...I couldn't control my laughter. "Seriously Naira, have you got a gym membership for yourself?" I was still laughing aloud.

Naira did not utter a word for a moment. Then slowly her lips curled into a smile and that cute dimpled face told me innocently, "Yes, I got a gym membership, but not for me, it is for you."

Immediately my smile turned into dismay. My laughter disappeared into thin air. My eyes popped out, as if I had just been woken from my sleep and dragged into a wrestling match.

"Me?" I stressed on the word to be doubly sure.

"Of course you, Rihen," she still displayed her dimpled smile.

"I...er...really don't need to go to a gym...you know... I'm just fine." I didn't want to sound too desperate to avoid the gym membership, but I was trying my best to change her mind. But it wasn't happening.

"Look at this, here...huh," she hastily grabbed my belly fat and was showing it. I was now feeling embarrassed.

"Okay fine, I removed her delicate hands from my bulging tummy, whatever you say." I surrendered to her. I knew she was right. I had consistently gained weight over a period of time and I was not doing anything to reduce it. My once lean body had turned into a protruding figure. I was unfit from inside out. And Naira was helping me to get into the fit mode again. We went inside. One really feels ashamed of their bulging fat bodies when you see hot bodies, sculpted figures and toned muscles roaming around at the centre.

It had been five months since Naira was in Surat. Each day seemed like a blessing to me. Yes, I was going to the gym regularly and it also showed on my body, which had become lean once again. I had also started working regularly at my Dad's factory. Life seemed to be on the right track for me, all thanks to Naira.

I met Naira three-four times a week. I grew close to her with each passing day. But there were times when I would dream about Aaruhi. Then, I would suddenly wake up feeling hazy and puzzled. Sometimes I did think back to that dazed, unbelievable and sad period of my life when I thought everything had finished. Today, Naira had helped me fill the gap, she has nurtured my broken heart. But somewhere somehow, Aaruhi still occupied a place deep in my heart. She was still there at the back of my mind.

"Hey, lost again?" said a coarse voice on the other end of the screen.

"No...no...I'm still here." Naira and I had decided to talk to Karan on a video call. Since Naira had moved to Surat, we often did a group chat with Karan.

"So, how are you doing buddy?" I asked Karan.

"Not as good as you, since you have Naira with you." He winked at me.

"Oh, common Karan...don't start this again. So which Ad are you shooting now...huh? Or should I say which models have turned on your interest...hehe?" Naira joked with him.

"Too many...Naira....ahh...just too many...which one would you like to know about...the one with curly hair or the one with deep eyes or the tall one or..."

"None," pat came Naira's reply.

I could make out the pangs of jealousy in her voice.

"Oh...why don't I show you my latest shoot photos? You can have a look at all my beautiful models there," Karan went on. He turned his mobile screen towards the laptop and opened a folder with lots of photos. There were photos of all kinds of models, but all of them were males. There was just one family photo with a female model and a cute kid. Rest were all Ad shoots of a menswear brand.

"So now tell me, which one do you like, Naira...the guy with curly hair or the deep eyes or the tall guy...you can choose. If you even want to meet any of them, come down here I'd be happy to introduce them to you." Now Karan was sounding serious.

"'Of course not Karan...you know I was kidding...I was talking about female models. These guys are too good for me. Besides I have you and Rihen, isn't it?" Saying this she nudged me. "Why don't you say something, Rihen?"

I didn't speak anything. Whenever we were on a group chat, it was mostly Karan and Naira who did most of the talking and joking, while I liked being the silent spectator. Actually, I could see a certain spark between them. Naira and Karan were always comfortable and shared jokes whenever they talked to each other. I did feel jealous of them sometimes, knowing Karan had a liking for Naira. But then I brushed away that thought knowing that we three were thick friends and nothing ought to come between us.

But the storm was already coming in our direction. Yes, we were unaware then, but the storm was going to create havoc in our lives. It was just a matter of time.

17

The Last Confession

The sky was dark and the winter air was already chilling up outside, giving me shivers as I waited for Naira outside the girl's hostel gate. As she approached, I could breathe a sort of nice and delicious flowery scent which provided warmth to my body.

"You are looking cute!" I exclaimed when I saw her clad in a cosy baby pink coloured fleece jacket and blue jeans.

"Thank you Rihen," her dimpled smile melted my heart. "And you are looking fit!" she chuckled at me. I had worn a fairly informal outfit. Grey trousers, a nice body fitting T-shirt and sneakers, nothing very jazzy for a fun date night.

"Obviously, isn't that the reason we are celebrating and going out for dinner tonight," I retorted.

"Yes, of course...and then there's something else too," she gave me a mysterious look. I wondered what other reason there could be.

"You are shivering. I can warm you up. Do you want me to cuddle you? My jacket can make you warm. Come." Naira took a step forward.

"We should be going," I said with a little start. "I'm already hungry. Our dinner is waiting."

"Oh again, you and your food and, what's the rush?" Naira called out as I hastened towards my car parked a few meters away. "We have got the whole night."

Looking at my panic-stricken face, she laughed loudly and gestured me to chill. "I'm just kidding, Rihen."

We drove to a nice multi-cuisine restaurant– Masala Stories- in the heart of the city. The restaurant had been finalised after a lot of debate. I wanted to eat non-veg food but Naira was keen on delicious veg food only. After a lot of deliberation, we finally decided on the newly opened Masala Stories Restaurant because it served both veg and non-veg. We had heard good reviews about the place that the taste and quality of food was superb and even the ambience was amazing. So, I told Naira why not try a new restaurant.

On the way, Naira was as usual blabbering about what they had been taught in class, which girl was her competitor in college, who broke up, who hooked up with whom, her usual hostel food complaints and on and on she went. I liked listening to her constant chatter. She would stop now and then and ask my opinion and I would avoid giving them. I told her how my day went.

As we entered Masala Stories, I could see a small crowd of people waiting outside the restaurant. As we were walking along, Naira slid her hand into mine. I felt her slender fingers gently caressing my palm. I turned to face her in the lamplight, my heart beating fast. So far, the evening seemed to be going like a dream. We walk on again, smiling at each other. Naira's shoulder brushed against mine. My entire body seemed to be on fire but, somehow, I managed to control my emotions. I could feel my breath thickening, but neither of us said a word.

We stopped at the restaurant entrance, waiting for our turn. Finally, our turn came and we went inside. The interiors of the restaurant were beautifully designed with comfortable seating and soft lights giving a romantic ambience to the whole place. We went and sat at a nice cosy corner just besides a window.

We ordered an exotic veg pizza with extra cheese, Manchow soup and burnt garlic fried rice. She joked for me to go easy on the cheese or I would again put on weight.

"No chance. If I do, no more pizzas for me ever again," I challenged her.

She giggled at the thought.

"Nice shirt, by the way," she told me.

"Oh thanks," I gave her a sheepish smile.

It seemed a perfect evening. A scent of fresh orchids filled the air. Jazz music was playing gently in the background. After a long time, I felt so content in life.

After we placed our order, we again played Rapid Fire on the table with a bottle, like we had done earlier during our trek. But this time, Naira changed the rules and declared that the winner of the game would get to ask five questions.

We started playing the game and both of us took turns taking a dare and tried our best to complete it to the satisfaction of the other. However, in the end, Naira won the game, giving a wicked smile.

"So Rihu, I get to ask you five rapid questions, huh?" Naira smirked at me.

"Well yes," I replied. "Shoot" I added.

"You need to reply honestly and quickly, it's a rapid fire round," she held my hand resting on the table.

"I'll see," I answered without looking directly at her.

"Okay, so here goes your first question. Love without selfishness..." she asked.

"Mom," I answered.

"Forgiveness or Punishment?" she put forth her next question.

"Emptiness," I replied.

"When you saw me the first time..." she blurted out the third question.

"Simple...Naira is a beautiful girl next door," I didn't want to sound too obvious about her.

"Okay, next question, during the trek what did you think of me?" she blabbered.

"The most different and amazing person I had ever met," I replied instantly.

"And my last question, what am I to you now?" she asked this very coyly.

"You have become a habit," I looked directly into her eyes and replied.

She had tears in her eyes.

I continued, "You know very well Naira that my eyes and I have got addicted to seeing you daily."

Just then, the live band in the restaurant started playing. After one song, Naira requested them to let her sing and they obliged. She sang a few lines of the song, *'Ek haseena se yun mulakat hogayi'*. Now I was moved. I felt very strongly motivated. The emptiness had been filled by her presence.

The waiter brought our food at that moment. As the waiter served our food, I suddenly noticed Naira's unusually huge backpack lying beside her on the sofa. "Are you planning to go directly to your class tomorrow morning or what?" I said pointing to her big bag.

"Why not, if you spend the whole night with me, I can directly go to my class in the morning." She winked at me.

The waiter stiffened a little and after serving our food, he quickly left our table.

"I don't mind," even I joined her in the joke. "By the way, the backpack reminds me of our camping trip, isn't it?"

"Ah yes, good old days. We met at the first camping adventure in Dang. You remember?" Naira questioned me.

"No, I hardly remember you at all. Yes, there were some other pretty girls I had my eyes on." I remarked.

"Obviously, why would you notice me? After all I had nothing special," she retorted.

"Jealous huh..." I laughed at her.

"Of course not. But tell me, did you really not notice me?" Naira looked at me questioningly.

I just chuckled.

"Tell me...no Rihen," she insisted.

"Ok...ok...I noticed the girl sleeping on the upper berth in the train journey to Shimla. I recognised you from our first trip. How can one not notice your cute dimples? You are as beautiful as a daisy in the morning sun. And I am a fan of your dimpled smile." I pinched her cheeks lightly. "Happy now? You girls are so hard to please, always longing for more compliments." I told her smilingly.

"So, when are you planning your next camping adventure?" she asked me, ignoring my last remark.

"Sometime next year, this time again to a different place, you will be joining right?" I scooped a pizza slice and looked at her.

"If you are there then yes, I'm in," she nodded and sipped her cold drink. "I'm sure even Karan will join us, that is if he gets time from his shoots," she smirked.

Karan...sometimes that guy gave me pangs of jealousy. He was our friend, but I knew his feelings for Naira too well. And he was somehow always present in our conversations.

"Even I think he will be too busy with his assignments. Let's see what happens when we do plan our next trip." With that I took another slice of pizza.

"You have become slim and trim, but it doesn't mean you can keep gorging on junk food." Naira stopped my hand.

"Just this last piece...I have a cheat day only once in a while...isn't it?"

"Er...well...yes..." she let go of my hand.

Once we finished our Pizza, we ordered some Brownies. While waiting, she rummaged in her backpack and asked me to close my eyes.

I looked curiously at what she was doing in her bag, but she pushed me away.
"Just close your eyes, will you?" she snapped at me.

I acted like I had closed my eyes. They were partly open and I saw her taking out a shiny parcel in wrapping paper. As she turned towards me, I quickly closed my eyes. Hmm...a gift for me. I thought to myself. Maybe it's again something to do to maintain my weight, a gift to make me stay healthy. I might have even thought she could have brought dumbbells or a skipping rope or some kind of fitness equipment for me.

She stretched out my hand and told me to open my eyes. She handed me a tiny present wrapped in frilly heart ribbon. It was light in weight. It certainly couldn't be dumbbells. Thank God.

"What is it? A fit bit watch?" I grinned at her.
"Just open it, will you," she looked at me lovingly.
I unwrapped the little present and a chain with a heart-shaped locket fell into my hand. It had a picture of the mountains.
"It reminded me of the first time we met," Naira said, her lips curving into a bright smile.
"It's fantastic. Thank you so much," I whispered into her ear.

"I want to say something, Rihen...well...er..." she paused for a few seconds.

"I love you Rihen, and want to spend the rest of my life with you. I have already told you before. I'm telling you again." She touched my hand, then came closer.

I swallowed a big chunk of the Brownie. I knew it in my heart all along, but this sudden revelation again was unexpected. I had somehow escaped this conversation on the mountains and now it had come up again.

Okay...just calm down. I told myself. She's not serious. Obviously, she's not serious. It's just a joke on me.

But her face revealed something else. I could feel her eyes on me, but I turned my head away from her scrutiny.

"I'm waiting for your answer. You don't want to reply?" she asked me at last, leaning towards me and putting her arms around me.

I felt nice. I was in a happy state, momentarily. I wished I could stay in her warm tender arms forever. But alas! I know it was not possible. It was true that I had developed strong feelings for Naira. Yes, I loved her too. But I could not confess to her. The Aaruhi episode had been too harsh for me. I wanted to move on, but I could not fully get Aaruhi out from my mind. This would be an injustice towards Naira. Yes, I loved Naira. But I was stuck in between, like in a quicksand. I wanted to reach out for Naira's hand but I was getting sucked into the quicksand, unable to release myself from the muck.

"Rihen," she nudged me and it brought me to the present.

"You don't want to talk about it, do you?" she was feeling impatient.

I just looked at her and did not reply.

Naira exhaled sharply. "Look Rihen, I know you have had a bad experience. But please forget Aaruhi. She is not part of your life anymore. You have to move on. She does not exist for you."

How could I explain to her that Aaruhi was still a part of my existence. As I looked towards her and met her steady gaze, I felt a sudden pull inside my chest. I wanted to unburden everything. I wanted to hug her, cry in her arms and just lay there besides her. But I couldn't bring myself to do that. Of all the people, I knew I could trust Naira. She had been so supportive of me. She could understand me with all my worries and feelings, she knew me so well just like a life partner. But I knew the answer to her question was not me.

"So, are you going to say something now or just keep quiet?" Naira was baffled by my behaviour.

At last, I broke my silence and uttered "It's too nice a night to spoil with the miserable tales of my life. I'll answer your question later."

"No, that is not fair Rihen. I want an answer now." Naira pleaded.

"If you insist then listen, I will not marry until Aaruhi gets married. I will settle down in life only after she does." I closed my eyes, trying to ignore the stab of pain inside my heart.

For a moment, she didn't move. Then very slowly she moved away from me, her face expressionless.

"Right. Got it," was all she said and then she became silent. It appeared to me like the calm before the storm. I could see a huge tornado coming.

She became teary-eyed.

"I cannot be with you until Aaruhi is completely out of my mind and soul. I wish to see her get settled." My voice shook a little. Then I tried to move closer to Naira.

"I'm sorry. I didn't mean to hurt you. Are you okay Naira?" I handed her a paper napkin to wipe her tears.

"I'm fine," she said matter-of-factly.

"I know you loved her very much. But this can't go on. There's nothing left between you two so, why do you wish to see her get settled. I don't understand you. We have been spending so much time together. I thought by now you would accept me in your life. I came down to your city just to be with you, to ease your pain so that you could forget Aaruhi. What is wrong with you? Don't you love me? Am I just your friend, nothing else?" Naira went on non-stop.

"It's not that." I protested.

"Then what is it?" she demanded.

I felt a sudden rage towards her for not understanding my situation and not supporting my decision.

She also got more aggressive. "Rihen, your ego is bigger than the mountains. You also love me but don't want to accept me. You are still living in the past, still thinking of the girl who ditched you. You are living in a state of denial…it's time to start living a life of your own, OK?"

She moved further away from me, tears trickling down her rosy cheeks.

"But I guess you are right, Rihen," she shrugged.

"I think it's getting late. We should leave," saying this she wiped her tears, brushed off my arms and got up from her seat.

By the end of our night, we just had half a plate of chips, a share of the veg pizza, a glass of cold drink each and plenty of emotional conversation.

The drive back was in total silence, only the sound of the car engine roaring could be heard. This wasn't the way things were supposed to go. We were supposed to have a lovely time tonight. Instead, here we were, sitting cross-faced in the car, not saying a word or even looking at each other. What should have been a most spectacular time for us ended with a heavy feeling?

Soon, we reached her hostel. When finally, she looked up, her expression choked my heart.

"Goodbye," Naira muttered softly and ran hurriedly towards the hostel gate.

"Goodbye," I called after her, but I'm not sure she heard. Naira was already at a distance, her shadow disappearing into the hostel building.

Naira vanished into the dark night.

I felt a deep feeling of despair. Maybe I had just ruined everything in my life.

When I had seen Naira the first time, when I saw her smile, my heart had forgotten that it was broken. And now today she was gone.

A few days later I got a call from Karan. He sounded very angry on the phone.

"Hello Karan," I said.

"I don't know what happened between you and Naira," He started off, no greetings, no friendliness, which was unlike Karan.

"What is the matter between you two? And I don't even want to know but I just want that you leave her as soon as possible. Keep away from her and forget her. In fact, I would advise you to forget both of us. Leave us alone. We don't want your friendship."

Without waiting for my explanation or my reply, Karan disconnected the call. It was the last I heard from him.

I had already made the biggest mistake of my life by loosing Naira, but I would never make the mistake of forgetting her.

I want to be your shadow,
So that wherever you go
I am always with you!

18

The Wedding

The whole wedding scene looked surreal. And the to-be bride's smile said it all. She was looking absolutely gorgeous. The red bindi, the mang tikka, and her subtle make-up made her face glow. There she stood, dressed in a beautiful red and green bandhini lehenga choli. The stylish green bandhini choli was complimented by her flared red bandhini lehenga and a net translucent red dupatta with border. The lehenga choli accentuated her curves perfectly and made her look like a princess. She radiated so much love and happiness on her special day. There were happy vibes all around.

I couldn't help smiling at this beautiful girl standing in the garden, posing for her wedding shoot. I so wanted to go there and wrap her tightly in my arms, kiss her forehead and just lay my head on her lap...Just then the photographer asked her to give a different pose and she did. Like me, several photographers too had their eyes only on her. I gazed at her in a loving and caring way. The photographers were capturing the beauty and shyness of the bride-to-be with their lens.

"Oh my God, look at you...you look like a diva...I love you Naira," saying this Karan, the bridegroom, came and hugged her. She hugged him back and they smiled at each other.

Yes, I was gate crashing Naira and Karan's wedding. Of course, I was formally invited, well because each of us was aware about the past. But I couldn't face them upfront. Instead, I sneaked in at their wedding. After all, it was the wedding of my two best friends - Karan and Naira and I had to attend it. I had disguised myself as a distant cousin of the bridegroom and was wearing a traditional outfit so that no one would doubt me.

The venue was a premium wedding lawn on the outskirts of Vadodara city. The sprawling lawn was decorated beautifully with natural scenery and an artificial pond, purple and blue orchids, water fountains, lantern-lit pathways, net panelling embellished with mirrors. The whole venue looked stunning and the atmosphere was filled with laughter and happiness. Overall, it was an elegant and lavish celebration.

From a distance I could sense that they were both so filled with love and complemented each other so well. Karan looked handsome in his bridegroom's outfit. He was wearing a maroon and cream sherwani with a red and green *paghdi* which matched Naira's outfit. The couple had chosen a vibrant colour palette for their D-day and both looked ravishing in their outfits.

It was heart-warming to see some very quiet and sweet moments between the bride and the groom. They looked so much in love that I could hardly believe this was the same Naira who had proposed to me.

"Naira, put your arms on his waist not on his face," the photographer was directing her for the correct pose. "Yes, Mr Photographer," Naira then shifted the position of her hands and stared right into Karan's eager eyes. She naughtily stepped hard on his toes with her heels. Karan yelled.

"My future wife, you just wait till the photo session is over." Saying this, Karan in return mischievously tickled Naira. They were completely lost in each other.

(Flashback)

I got lost in my own thoughts. They took me back to when I was attending Lakshya's wedding in Udaipur. He had invited all the group members for his destination wedding. This was before Naira had proposed to me in the restaurant.

Karan couldn't make it because of his work commitments. However, Naira and me were free at that time and decided to go together to the wedding. All the guests from the groom's side had to assemble at Ahmedabad, from there a Volvo coach would take everyone to Udaipur. We were also among them. Lakshya was travelling to Udaipur in his car with his parents. I couldn't stop thinking about that trip and remembered each moment spent with Naira. Unlike the last bus trip during our trek from Chandigarh to Manali where I had avoided Naira, this time I was with Naira during the entire bus journey. Those rare moments were very precious to me. During those two days at the wedding, I could sense

Naira flirting with me. She would always come and stand near me, even eat from my plate and pass me compliments.

Since it was a destination wedding, arrangements had been made for the guests to stay at a beautiful resort in Udaipur. All the members from the trekking group were given two adjacent rooms. There was a pool party in the evening, puja the next morning followed by the wedding and the reception party at night. Naira never left my side during the whole time. She would wait for me to join her at the different functions, sit next to me in the group, cracked funny jokes when we were all together. I could feel her stealing glances in my direction whenever she could, and when I would look back at her, she would just smile. What a wonderful time we had together.

When Lakshya and his bride were doing their wedding shoot, all of us (trekking group) were watching them from a distance. Naira and the others were passing funny comments while the bride and the groom were giving different poses. Standing near me, she said, "I would never do such poses, would you Rihen?" I shrugged my shoulders.

"My wedding would be simple and I will only click a few photos. This is all too fancy. How would you like your wedding to be?"

I only half listened to her and did not reply to any of her questions. Thankfully the photo-shoot ended and it was time for the wedding to begin. When Lakshya arrived with the *Baarat* on a huge brown horse, everyone cheered him.

Again, Naira commented, "Riding a horse is very old fashioned. If you marry me, come on a bike."

I turned to face her and gripped her shoulders, "Naira, we are not getting married."

"Why not," she retorted in a shrill voice.

"Because in the beginning everyone thinks that he or she is different, but at last they are all the same."

"No dear, everyone is not the same," Naira said in a defensive tone.

"I know you love me but you are afraid that I will leave you like Aaruhi left you. I have told you so many times and I have waited too long. Now I can't wait anymore, my uncle and Mom are forcing me to settle down. Every day they are sending me pictures of different boys for marriage."

"Well, then settle down. Why wait for me?" my voice became stiff.

"Okay, fine I will wait for 15 days then I will do what you want. If you tell me to get married to Karan then I will because I love you so much that I will do anything for you," saying this Naira shook her head in despair.

"Look Naira, Karan is a good guy. He is more practical than me. And you know him well. He is a suitable partner for you. I'm sure of that. Please trust my decision. And get married to Karan. I don't love you and I'm not the right person for you. I know everyone is selfish, I am too and my selfishness is to see you happy. I know you will be happy with him." I immediately wanted to bite my lip, to disappear somehow into thin air, to take back what I had said. For a while there was silence, except for the distant chanting of wedding mantras at the end of the garden.

"I will do whatever you want me to do. I will marry Karan and one day you will realise what you have lost."

She was silent for a moment, fiddling with her dupatta. When at last she looked up, her expression choked me.

"Bye," she said quiet voice and walked away from me.

After the wedding we came back to Surat and slowly resumed our normal life. We went back to being friends and I hoped that Naira had forgotten our conversation at Lakshya's wedding. I thought all that was behind us and we had moved past it. I was sure that Naira had given up any hopes of marrying me.

But I was mistaken and Naira brought up the subject again at the restaurant where things had gone from bad to worse. That evening had been a disaster and we both had parted with a lot of unhappiness and disappointment.

Those two conversations were coming to my mind today. After that day at the restaurant, we never met or talked on the phone. And here today I was witnessing her marriage to Karan.

(Coming back to the present)

Karan came to the wedding riding a bike, as wished by Naira. He was on a bullet, wearing a traditional maroon and cream coloured sherwani and dark glares. He looked like a hero, and his entry was really filmy.

During the *Varmala* ceremony, the *Baarati's* lifted Karan up so the bride's side also lifted Naira up. It was a grand affair and everyone seemed to be thoroughly enjoying themselves.

The melodious sound of the wedding band filled my ears. I looked around and realised I had reached the *Mandap* where Naira and Karan's wedding was taking place. From a distance, I could see the happy faces of the bride and the groom sitting in the *Mandap*. Friends and relatives surrounded them. There was happiness and laughter in the hall. I was happy that she was happy. Although, I still couldn't believe that they both were getting married, but I was happy for them.

Karan filled Naira's head with *Sindhoor* and tied the *Mangalsutra* around her neck. And in those few moments, everything just changed. From Naira Sharma, she became Mrs Naira Shukla. Karan who was single a few moments ago was now a married man. A few hours ago, Naira was that simple and cute natured loving, working girl. But now she was someone's wife and had a responsibility towards her new family. While the guests were having their lunch, Karan and Naira came out from the *Mandap* towards the lawn and they spotted me before I could move from there.

"Congratulations to both of you. Wish you a happy married life," was all I could manage.

"Thank you," both replied in unison.

"Naira, if Karan or anyone ever bothers you, just let me know."

She just nodded her head.

I looked at Karan, "Just remember, if she is ever hurt then you can't even imagine what I will do."

They shook my hand as a mark of our friendship. It was the last time we three held each other's hands this way.

I did not have the courage to stay there any longer. I bid goodbye to the smiling couple. I walked slowly away from the venue. Life had come a full circle again. I was happy and sad at the same time. I fell in love with Aaruhi but had been betrayed by her. My broken heart was nursed by Naira who fell in love with me. But I did not wish to reciprocate her feelings. I knew Karan also liked Naira a lot. So, I let her go. Because deep down, I knew my wounded heart would not be able to give her the same love and I did not want her to forever nurse my feelings. I knew Karan would be an ideal partner for her. He was more practical. I was an emotional fool. Karan would keep her happy no matter what. And a sweet innocent girl like Naira needed a rock not a weeping pillow.

The first time I was completely and madly in love with Aaruhi. They say love makes you blind and I was definitely a fool to fall for such a girl, for whom love was just a game, and I was just another card in her game, a means to an end. She had played her game well, though I had also been swooned by her beauty, by her charming talks and by her false emotions. How stupid of me! I did not think about anything else and was swayed by her sweet talks. I learnt my lesson the hard way. Fate had given me a hard blow in my face. And she left...left without saying a word...left in an instant...without saying goodbye...without a word...

leaving an empty space for me to cry in, left in despair, all alone, heart-broken, wounded, unhealed, hollow...as if only I had all the sorrow in the world.

But then Naira came into my life. She was not the love of my life. But she gave me the support I needed to come out of this hole. She held me at my lowest. She cared for me, she nourished me, she brought me back to my senses. In the process, yes, I developed feelings for her, I have a soft corner for her. And I knew that she did too. I knew she had feelings for me. But I also knew that if I rejected her, she will move on in her life. I was not brave to love someone a second time. They say, "He who has once burnt his mouth always blows his soup." And life had taught me well. I had learned the hard way and experienced a painful lesson in love, one which I can never forget. Naira taught me many things in life. I need to learn to move on, so that I can lead a fulfilling life.

Maybe the time is not right for me to move on.

Maybe I am a coward for admitting my feelings to Naira.

Maybe I will not be able to bear any heartbreak again.

Maybe my heart doesn't want to start feeling love again.

Maybe God has someone else in mind for me.

Maybe my life is meant for travel.

There are so many maybe's...And then there is that one maybe...

Maybe I could have lived a happy life with Naira after all, had I accepted her proposal.

Was Naira happy with Karan?

Was my decision to reject Naira's proposal wrong?

What if I had said yes to Naira?

Would she have been happier with me?

These questions come again and again to my mind. I can't stop thinking about her. Like a whirlpool, these questions keep revolving in my head. I couldn't sleep properly because of these questions. I just wanted to find out if Naira was happy with Karan. I tried several times but without any luck. Naira and Karan, both had blocked their social media profiles, keeping it a private account so even that option was closed to me. I knew they were going to stay in Vadodara after their marriage but that was it. I had no further information about either of them. All time my heart was just longing to be with her, to feel her presence, to experience her warmth, to hold her, to embrace her and just be with her.

Epilogue

You Met Me for a Reason

I am sitting alone on a bench on Platform no. 2, waiting for my train to arrive. Off on another trekking trip, on another journey, to a new destination. This was my fifth trekking trip and this time I was off to Kedarkantha trek. I'm quite excited. My energy levels are as high as during my first and second trekking trips. There are goose bumps on my hands, my feet are shaking and my heart is thumping loudly with the excitement of the upcoming adventure.

Three years have passed since Naira got married. I often wonder how their life must be after marriage. She hasn't been in touch with me. Neither has Karan. But I still think of her, or rather think of them. Life hasn't really moved on for me post her marriage but I guess I am surviving. Many times, I sit back and go through everything that happened in my life in the past few years. I was a free bird, always talkative, and ever smiling. I had always been passionate about trekking. It was my first love. I liked to travel to new places, explore the unknown and trek through the mountains. Trekking gave me an adrenaline rush like nothing else. It made me happy and content. As if I was made for the mountains.

Suddenly, the blaring horn of the incoming train disturbs my thoughts. The train doesn't stop at this station and passes at high speed. Few minutes later another train arrives and stops at the platform. I can see quick movement of people jumping in and out of the train. It also leaves the platform in ten minutes. I stretch my hands up in the air. My train is half an hour late so I have no other option but to while away my time at the station. Feeling hungry, I buy samosas from the vendor nearby and again sit on the bench while gorging on them. I had just taken a bite when the loud whistle of another train shook me. I continued eating my samosa. The train slowed down and stopped. It was an express train. I took the last bite of my samosa and looked up towards the train. And my eyes couldn't believe what I saw. My eyes popped out, my hands shook in surprise and I literally gulped down the last bite of samosa.

She stepped out of the train and was pulling out the luggage from the train carriage. She was just a few feet away from me. The next instant, Naira also looked up and saw me. At first her face turned blank as if she has seen a ghost, then slowly she came towards me. I quickly cleared my mouth of the ketchup and samosa crumbs smeared on my face with my T-shirt sleeves. It feels like a dream seeing Naira step out of the train and coming towards me.

She comes near me and asks, "Hi Rihen, how are you? Long-time"

She called me Rihen and not Rihu like she used to call me previously.

"Hello," I mumbled. That's all I could manage. I didn't know what else to say. I was dumbstruck.

"How are you Naira," I asked her after a pause of a few moments. Before she could reply, I saw Karan coming out of the train, carrying two more suitcases with him.

She turned around and shouted to him, "Karan, please look after Rihu."

Now, I was astonished. Why did she ask Karan to look after me? What was she thinking?

I was extremely puzzled and did not understand what she meant. On the other hand, Karan went back towards the carriage and stood near the steps. He held out his hand to a little boy who carefully stepped down the steps and jumped playfully on the platform.

What a cute little boy! I thought to myself.

Karan held his hand and they were both coming towards us. When the boy came closer, his facial features were very similar to Naira. The little boy also had cute dimples on his cheeks.

"Rihen, meet my son Rihu," Naira told me.

"And Rihu, this is Rihen uncle. He shares your name." She said to her son.

'Rihen, Rihu?? Really?'

I was speechless. I couldn't even mutter a word or say Hi to little Rihu. I just shook his hands and hugged him. I didn't know how to react, what to say. I was utterly shocked. This little boy was the son of Karan and Naira and they had named him Rihu. After my name. Seriously? Was I still important to them? After so much time had passed, after all these years, suddenly one day I bump into Naira, Karan and their son named Rihu. Life seemed to have again come a full circle right before my eyes.

Looking at my bewilderment, Naira and Karan both smiled at each other. Karan nodded to Naira to speak up.

"It wasn't so easy to forget you Rihen," Naira started talking.

"If it wasn't for Karan and his immense support, I would have led a miserable life. After you rejected my proposal, I got closer to Karan and soon we decided to turn our friendship into a lifetime partnership. We were not soul mates but we were good friends. And this helped blossom our relationship. Today, I am thankful that I married Karan and we both are very happy with each other." She glanced lovingly at Karan who came by her side and embraced her.

"But..." she continued.

"I did think of you and our special bond many times and even Karan was aware about it. You didn't stay in touch with us and left our lives without a word. But God gave me a piece of you in another way. A gift I'll cherish forever. When I delivered a baby boy, both of us knew what name we were going to give him." Tears welled up in her eyes.

"And here is our little Rihu, named after the very special person in my life Rihen." She wiped her tears.

"He is everything to me now. And is just like you."

"Me?" I asked in astonishment.

"Yes, you," this time Karan replied.

"He is a bit reserved like you and loves going out, travelling and has an adventurous streak within him. So, he reminds us of you in every way, every single day." Karan and Naira shared this together.

When I looked at Naira, I could see that same old smile on her face and this really relaxed me. Karan also looked comfortable and the initial awkwardness amongst us was gone.

"So, Rihen where are you off to?" Karan changed the topic.

"This time it's Kedarkantha. My fifth Trekking Trip." I replied enthusiastically. All the worries of the past had been forgotten. I was now excited about my upcoming adventure.

"Cool, buddy. This is my number," saying this Karan gave me his card.

"Stay in touch with us now and suggest us some good treks." He told me.

"Yes, definitely," and I shook his hands. Then I hugged both of them. Finally, after so many years, I could relax as if a big burden had been lifted from my shoulders.

After bidding our goodbyes, we set off in different directions towards our own life journeys.

Now I understood the real reason of why I met Naira. She came into my life to teach me that not every girl is Aaruhi. There are also girls like Naira, who healed my wounded heart with her selfless love and care. Now, I also knew that my life's mission was to travel and make new memories. I travel and encourage others also to do the same - Travel once in a year to a place where there is no phone connectivity or internet and meet yourself, discover your inner self.

> *If you believe that Love is only about being with someone,*
> *Then you will never understand the true meaning of Love.*

* * * * * * *

Acknowledgement

First and foremost, I would like to thank God, the Almighty for showering His blessings on me throughout my life and more importantly to complete my novel.

I would like to express my gratitude to all those people who have been a great support to me through my entire journey as a writer. My parents, family and friends who have been my strength in whatever I have done and achieved in my life. They have encouraged me to write this book. My sister, Nishita Jariwala has been a constant source of inspiration in everything I do.

My special thanks to my Co-author Mayuri Talia. She is the Author of the novel 'Tears of My Heart,' and also a full-fledged Content Writer. From reading early drafts to writing and editing the chapters, to giving me advice and guiding me in everything, she played an important part in helping me to complete this book.

Finally, thanks to the entire team of White FalconPublishing who helped me so much. I am thankful to Nancy Gupta, my Publishing Manager and the editor, Renu Arya for their inputs and help through each step of the publishing and printing process.

I would also like to make a special mention to all my readers! Thank you and Stay Connected with me.

CPSIA information can be obtained
at www.ICGtesting.com
Printed in the USA
LVHW101801310722
724828LV00021B/306